Breakfast with the Alien
and Other Short, Short Stories

Breakfast with the Alien
and Other Short, Short Stories

By Greg Roensch

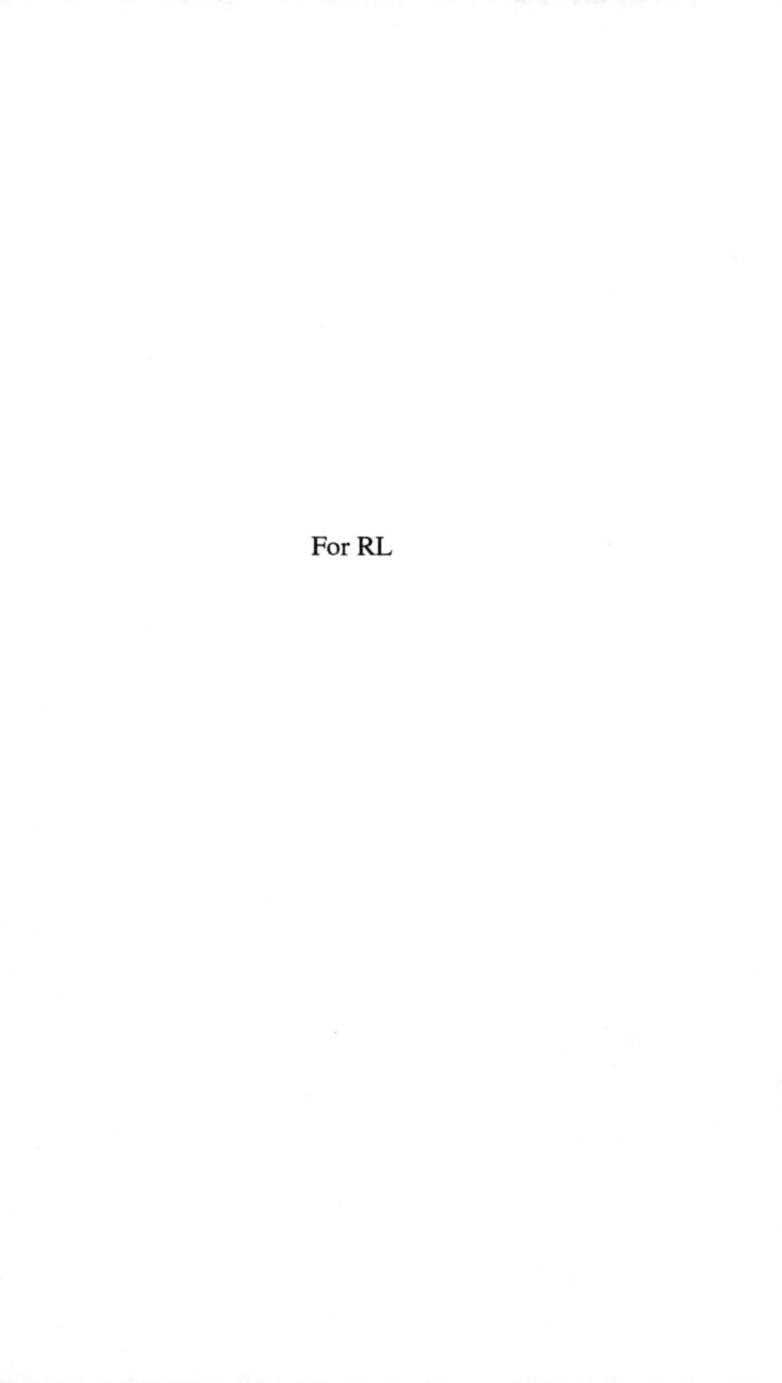

For RL

Go, litel bok, go ...

– Geoffrey Chaucer, *Troilus and Criseyde*

Contents

Breakfast with the Alien

Max Marsupolis can't believe he's sitting at the breakroom table across from an alien. The extraterrestrial blinks rapidly, his turquoise-green eyes studying Max as if he's met his kind before. Max reaches his hand across the table and introduces himself, though he senses the alien doesn't understand a word.

The alien sits and blinks as Max attempts to engage him in small talk.

"Is this your first day?"

"It's supposed to be cooler this week."

"Have you been to the new mall yet?"

"Traffic this morning sure was a nightmare."

No response. Nothing. Just more blinking of those turquoise-green eyes. Max thinks about his favorite alien movies. *E.T.*, *Close Encounters of the Third Kind*, *The Man Who Fell to Earth*, *The Day the Earth Stood Still*. The alien doesn't look like any of the aliens in those movies. In fact, he looks a lot like Johnny Depp in *Edward Scissorhands*, except for the eyes and the fact that he doesn't have scissorhands. It's the disheveled hair, thinks Max.

Max reaches for a doughnut hole from the pink cardboard box on the table and offers it to the creature sitting across from him. The alien doesn't make a move, but continues staring straight ahead with those rapidly blinking eyes. What do aliens eat, Max wonders? Do they like sweets? Are they vegetarians? Meat-eaters? At the thought of "meat-eaters," the alien shifts his gaze to Max's fingers and licks his thin brown lips. A sticky string of dark-blue saliva streams down his chin and pools on the table near the napkin dispenser. He's reading my mind, thinks Max as he pops the doughnut hole into his mouth and rests both hands in his lap. He chews but he isn't hungry anymore.

The buzzer sounds. Max and the alien both turn to look at the clock on the wall near the door.

"Time to get to work," says Max.

He stands, but the alien doesn't move. He's waiting for someone, thinks Max. Does anyone know he's here? Should I call Security? HR? Does he want to be taken to my leader?

"Nice to meet you," says Max. "Don't forget to drop by the mall when you have a chance."

Without thinking, Max extends his hand again before remembering the way the alien had eyed his meaty fingers. Balling his hands into tight, sweaty fists, Max moves away, worrying with each step that the alien will pounce. He's sweating heavily by the time he reaches the door.

In the hallway, Max nearly bumps into Alice Loverly, the longtime VP of Human Resources.

"What's the word, Max?" she asks. "You look like you've seen a ghost."

"Rough weekend," Max replies, "but I'll be alright after some more coffee."

"Sounds good. Anyone else in the breakroom?"

"Just some new guy," says Max. "He seems nice enough but kind of quiet."

Max notices the ultra-gloss, cherry-red polish on Alice's fingernails as she places her hand on the doorknob to enter the breakroom.

"I'll catch you later, Alice," Max says as he watches her enter the room. And then he whispers under his breath, "or maybe not."

She Only Whispers

There was a whisper on her lips, such a faint whisper I couldn't make out the words.

"What's that?" I asked, leaning closer.

She repeated whatever it was she'd been trying to say, but to no avail. Perhaps she was mute, and mouthing the words in some other setting might have been accompanied by an elaborate and well-practiced series of hand gestures. Or maybe I'd lost my hearing overnight.

I snapped my fingers near both ears. The crisp pop came in loud and clear. And if I'd been thinking clearly I wouldn't have needed to conduct an impromptu hearing test. The wind rustling though the trees near my campsite could have told me that much. Or the dull roar of an unseen airliner streaking across the gray early-morning sky.

What should I do now, I wondered? There was something frantic about the whispering woman, something panicked about the way she shot her eyes this way and that while trying to make me understand her words. What could I do – how could I help – if I didn't know what she was saying?

She reached into her jacket pocket as if looking for something – maybe a pen and paper, maybe a cellphone. She patted down the pockets of her well-worn jeans then looked around on the ground as if she'd misplaced something, a purse perhaps, or a backpack.

Where did she come from, this mysterious, whispering woman? I can't tell you much, other than that she stumbled into my camp last night as I was turning in. It scared the hell out of me at first; I thought she was a bear coming to raid my food supply. I relaxed, though, when she came through a break in the trees. My first thought was how frail she looked; she was but a wisp of a woman. I didn't have much time to think after that because she stumbled straight into my site and collapsed by the embers of the dying fire before either of us could utter a word.

I bent down to check if she was still breathing. She was, but she'd passed out, so I lifted her and carried her into my small tent. Indeed, I thought, she's just skin and bones. I draped my sleeping bag over her slumbering body and retreated outside to sleep by the fire pit. As I lay there, bundled in my old wool blanket, I dozed off thinking about the mysterious stranger and wondering what I'd learn in the morning.

I awoke the next day to the faint shuffle of feet. I must have fallen into a deep sleep because my skittish guest had already lit a fire to boil water for coffee.

"Good morning," I said.

She nodded and offered a nervous half-smile.

"You gave me quite a shock last night," I said. "I thought you were a bear."

She smiled again in the same way as before and shrugged her shoulders as if to apologize.

"It's alright," I said. "But you sure don't expect to see many people out here in the middle of the night."

That's when she whispered. I leaned forward, unable to decipher her meaning. After failing numerous attempts to make herself understood, the woman picked up a nearby stick and cleared a patch of dirt.

"Now you're on to something," I said, trying to encourage her. "Let's see what this mystery is all about."

With that, the frail woman with the nervous eyes bent down and scratched out a handful of words near the stone ring of the campfire. I couldn't make out her scribbled letters at first, but the message became clear as she scrawled the last letter and backed away.

"HELP ME," she'd written. "He's coming!"

And Then My Tooth Fell Out

I covered both hands over my mouth and let out a muffled groan. Holy crap, I thought, this hurts like hell. And then my tooth fell out. Sarah dropped the hammer that had just done a number on my upper lip and said, "Oh my god, honey. I didn't see you there."

I grabbed a bag of peas from the freezer and pressed it hard against my puffy, throbbing mouth. All I could think about was getting to the dentist – and fast. With my tooth in one hand and my car keys in the other, I told Sarah to stay with the kids while I rushed over to catch Dr. Duggins before he left for the day. He was a hard-working and, I must say, extremely good-looking man in a full-head-of-hair, all-American quarterback kind of way.

I was in luck when I rolled into the parking lot a few minutes past closing time. Dr. Duggins was still there, and after a quick look around my mouth, he agreed this couldn't wait. He led me to a chair, passed me a pair of orange-tinted goggles, and jabbed around the inside of my mouth with a long, slow needle full of Novocain.

"It's for the pain," he said.

"Thank God you're still here," I mumbled.

As he readied his tools, I thought back to the accident. Sarah had been tapping lightly on a picture frame before uncorking the full-armed backswing that set this whole mess in motion. I could have sworn she saw me coming up behind her.

"This shouldn't take too long," said Dr. Duggins, flashing his all-American quarterback smile, his full head of hair waving slightly in the artificial breeze of the office air-conditioning. He pressed a foot-switch and my chair reclined all the way back.

When my mouth was completely numb, Dr. Duggins poked at my gums to gauge the full extent of the damage. Once again, I flashed back to my wife and that wild swing of the hammer. I had to snicker at the absurdity of the situation. What else could I do?

"You need to stay still," said the dentist.

"Sorry," I said, my mouth stuffed with cotton and a suction tube hanging off my lip.

The mechanical whine of the dentist's drill seemed to come from farther away now. And I was very tired, like I might even fall asleep right here in the chair. At least I wasn't feeling any more pain. Then, through the orange-tinted lens of the goggles, I noticed the door swing open. Was I imagining things? Could it be? What's she doing here? In my semi-conscious, comfortably-numb state, I saw my wife's big, beautiful, toothy smile when she slipped into the room. Sarah had fixed up her hair and put on her makeup.

"How can you smile at a time like this?" I wanted to say. "Look at what you've done?"

I realized then that Sarah wasn't smiling at me as she cozied up to our handsome dentist and planted a long, deep kiss on his mouth.

Whatever that guy had shot me up with was working like gangbusters now. I couldn't move or say a thing, and soon I'd be out for good.

Folderol

"'Folderol,'" shouted the king. "'Folderol,' you say. That's balderdash. When I offer you a gift, a rare and priceless gift that's been passed down through my family for generations, it's a sign of royal affection. It's not be tossed away like scraps to the royal hounds."

"I meant no disrespect, my husband," replied the queen. "But surely your royal highness must realize that this ... this ..." She had a difficult time finding the words. "This object or any other object, precious though it may be, cannot so easily pay off your transgressions."

With that, the queen turned on her heels and stormed out of the throne room.

"Well that didn't go very well," said the king to the man who slipped out from behind an arras.

"Your majesty," said the man, "we seem to have misjudged the strength of your queen's character in such matters."

"Did you hear what she called my great-great-grandmother's pearl necklace?" the king bellowed. "She called it 'Folderol.'"

"Yes, sire. It was an unfortunate choice of words, but …"

"I'll tell you what's unfortunate, Sir Owen. It's unfortunate when the king's very own right-hand man and his most trusted confidante and advisor fails miserably in helping his king win back the heart of the queen. That's what's unfortunate."

"Yes, your highness, but …"

"Silence. If we don't have any better luck with the next attempt, I'm going to find someone who can provide better counsel. And quit interrupting me. I know perfectly well that my misconduct has turned the queen against me. But even you must admit that Princess Jasmina is pleasing to the eye, is she not?"

"Yes, your highness," said Sir Owen as he leaned closer to the king. "Perhaps your queen desires something more than a piece of jewelry, precious though it may be. Maybe there's something else we can do to regain her affection."

"Stop speaking in riddles, old man. Spit it out."

"Very well, my liege. Here's what I'm thinking," said Sir Owen. "Instead of offering her a valuable bauble, I suggest you deliver into her possession the head of her rival as just recompense for your past indiscretions."

The king looked agape at his counselor, shooting his eyes from left to right as was his habit when contemplating an idea that struck a chord with him. Turning toward Sir Owen, the king spoke in a hushed, conspiratorial voice.

"By all the gods, man, I think you're on to something. It's certainly a shame to snuff out the life of one so beautiful, one so young as Princess Jasmina. But I don't see any other way out of this torturous state of affairs. Let it be done discreetly," whispered the king, "let it be done."

Pygmalion

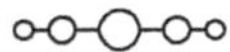

"Back off, buster. What are you doing?"

The sculptor gasped. "My prayers have been answered. You're alive!"

"Yes, I'm alive," said Galatea, the newly animated sculpture.

"But that means …" started Pygmalion.

"It means Venus granted your wish," finished the alabaster-skinned beauty. "But it doesn't give you free rein to place your gnarled paws all over me."

Galatea's words didn't register with the sculptor. He was dizzy with amazement over his marble creation come to life. "You're even more beautiful than I could have imagined." He walked toward her.

"Stop right there," said Galatea. "We need to get something straight."

"Yes my love. Anything you say." Pygmalion went to embrace his creation. "But first grant me just one kiss. I must feel the softness of your lips on mine."

When the sculptor was close enough, Galatea struck him on the cheek with a hard slap that echoed off the studio's high walls and halted Pygmalion in his lusty tracks.

"What was that for?" he asked. The force of the blow reminded him that Galatea was indeed made of stone.

"I told you we need to get something straight."

"Okay," said Pygmalion rubbing his cheek. "What?"

"While you've been lusting over my marble body," said Galatea, "and praying to Venus to bring me to life, I was unable to tell you that I don't share the same feelings for you." She let that sink in for a moment before making sure her meaning was clear. "I don't love you."

"What are you talking about?" said Pygmalion, feeling as if he'd been struck again by her stone palm. "How can you not love me? I made you."

"Indeed, you did. And I'm grateful for that. But if truth be told," said Galatea, "I'm more attracted to her." Galatea pointed at a newly chiseled statue of a busty young shepherdess, a minor figure Pygmalion was making for a manger scene at a local church.

"But ..." said the sculptor, "she's a peasant."

"That may be," replied Galatea, "but she's a lovely peasant."

With that, Galatea walked over to the base of the sculpture and knelt.

"Venus," she whispered, "hear my prayer ..."

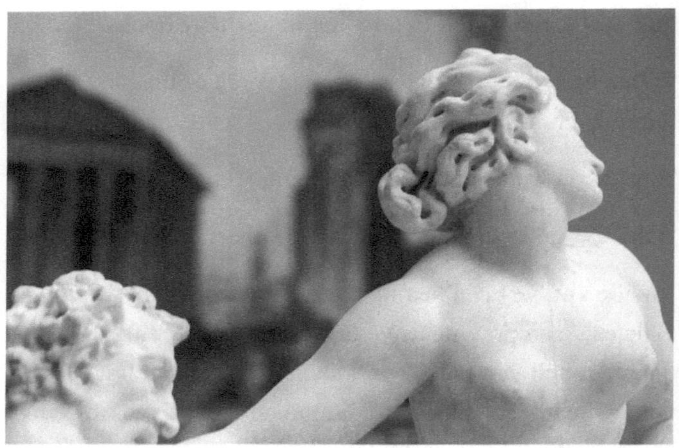

Blame Chernobyl

I blame Chernobyl. No, I wasn't there when the reactor
blew up. I was in Hamburg, more than 800 miles away,
and I recall huddling around the television with others at
the hostel as reporters described the size of the leak and
the wind patterns pushing the cloud in our direction. We're
fine, they told us, but stay inside when it rains – just to be
safe. And avoid fresh produce for the next few weeks.

After Hamburg, and after news of Chernobyl died down,
I roamed around Europe for a year. London. Amsterdam.
Paris. Barcelona. Pamplona. Those were just a few stops
on my Grand Tour. I made my way across the continent
by train and boat. I hitchhiked. I connected with strangers
and even traveled with some of them for a few days before
we'd go our separate ways. I was young. I was carefree. I
was naïve.

Not long after flying home to California, I got sick. My muscles ached. My eyelids were heavy. I felt like I had a fever even though my temperature was normal. And I had a constant bitter taste in my mouth. It's just the flu, I thought. It'll be gone soon enough.

I was right. The "flu" went away after a week.

Then it came back. I stayed in bed for two weeks to let the illness run its course. When I didn't get better, I went to the doctor, something I rarely did back in those days. "Your tests are all normal," he said. "Keep resting to give the bug time to work its way out of your system."

Looking back at the three decades since then, I've seen all sorts of doctors – all kinds of specialists. They listen. They probe. They poke. They test. They give advice. But they never find a cure for what ails me. Look at it this way, they say, it could be worse.

That's right, I think, it could be worse.

I've learned to live with the disease. I have good periods, months at time even, but it always comes back to lay me low all over again. The last doctor I saw, a chronic fatigue specialist, told me, "we all have to come to a point of acceptance."

"Thanks for nothing, doc," I wanted to say. That was my gut reaction, but part of me also understood where he was coming from. Every few months I get the achy muscles, the heavy eyelids, the fever that isn't a fever, and that bitter taste in my mouth, and for the next week or two I know what life has in store for me. This is my "normal." And until someone comes up with a better explanation, I blame Chernobyl.

The Cloud

"Fuck the cloud," said the lady with the magenta handbag. "And fuck you."

"I'm sorry, ma'am," replied the salesman wearing the powder blue vest. "I'm doing my best to help you, but is that language necessary?"

"Really?" said the woman. "How about this? You're an asshole. Do you like that language any better?"

"I know you're upset, but there's only so much I can do."

"You haven't done anything."

"Our specialists have taken a very close look. This is just one of those cases where technology let us down."

The woman stared hard at the salesman like she might leap across the counter and take a bite out of his jugular.

"If you read the online manual," continued the salesman. "This is exactly why we recommend at least two backups."

"You're a real piece of work," said the woman, swinging her handbag up onto the glass countertop. "The whole reason I put all my stuff on the cloud is because YOU told me it was foolproof."

"Excuse me, ma'am, but I would never say that."

"I'm talking about 'you' as in 'you people,'" replied the woman. "I'm talking about you scumbags, you jerkwads, you do-anything-to-make-a-sale motherfuckers."

"I'm truly sorry, ma'am, but you're going to have to leave now. There's nothing else we can do for you here."

"I want to see the manager."

The salesman looked around the store, thankful that there weren't any other customers in the computer department.

"I demand to see the manager," the woman said more loudly.

"I am the manager," said the salesman. "Here's what I can do for you. I'm sorry we can't retrieve your data, but I can give you a gift card for your next purchase."

"Ha," snorted the woman. "Next purchase? Do you really think I'm ever coming here again?"

"Ma'am, I …"

"Where's your boss? I want to see someone who's in charge here."

"He's out to lunch," said the salesman.

"Out to lunch?" snapped the woman. "You're all out to lunch."

"I'm going to call security now," warned the man.

"Go ahead," said the woman. "I'm not leaving until I get my stuff back."

"As I explained to you earlier," said the salesman, "your files were erased from the cloud when we tried to recover your hard drive last week. They're all gone and they aren't coming back."

"My work?"

"Gone."

"My photos?"

"Gone."

"My music?"

"Gone, gone, gone."

The lady reached into her magenta handbag and pulled out a silver-plated hammer.

"Wait …" said the salesman, but before he could utter another word, the woman swung the hammer hard on the plate glass countertop of the case displaying the latest smartphones.

"Fuck you," she said, turning to leave the store, "and fuck the cloud."

Dear Mr. Polar Bear

Dear Mr. Polar Bear,

I'm writing to say "hi" and to see how you're doing. I'm not sure you remember me, but I saw you on the last day of my trip to Svalbard. At the start of our Arctic cruise, the guides warned that we might not see any polar bears. "It's not like going to the zoo," said the team leader. As it turned out, there wasn't anything to worry about. We were lucky to see more than our fair share of bears while visiting your home above the Arctic Circle.

We saw all kinds of bears. Young. Old. Male. Female. We saw bears swimming through sea ice, rolling around on glaciers, and playfully begging for food from our kitchen staff. I don't remember each bear, but I remember you, Mr. Polar Bear. You were the last bear I saw on the trip. You were also the only bear I saw devouring the remains of a seal cub, its shredded red carcass staining the chunk of ice you were sitting on. As we left Svalbard behind, entering the Barents Sea for the crossing back down to the European mainland, I kept my binoculars trained on you until you disappeared out of sight.

That was nearly 10 years ago. Wow, time flies, Mr. Polar Bear. I haven't been back to the Arctic, but from all accounts things aren't looking too good for you guys up there. Global warming is melting the sea ice at an alarming rate, which is making it harder and harder for you to hunt for food. I'm wondering how you're getting along, Mr. Polar Bear. Have you changed your habits? Is it harder to catch fish, and seals, and other food? Do you make more of an effort when begging from the cruise ships? Are you starving, Mr. Polar Bear?

I read a recent news story about a team of Russian scientists who were trapped in their weather station by ten polar bears. Where you there? If not, maybe you know some of the bears who were involved. I read that one of the bears ate a dog at the weather station. I bet the scientists were worried that they might be next on the menu. You have to do what you have to do when you're hungry, right?

Anyway, Mr. Polar Bear, I'm sorry for going on so long, but I hope this letter finds you well. Please say "hi" for me to all the other polar bears up in Svalbard, as well as to any walruses, seals, whales, fish, birds, and other creatures you come across. I know you might want to eat them if you see them, but say "hi" for me anyway. I had a great time visiting your Arctic home ten years ago and I hope to see you again someday. Drop me a line if you have a few minutes. I'd love to hear from you.

And if you ever visit sunny California, you're always welcome to crash on the futon at our place. We can even put you up in the kids' room. You'll love them.

Okay, that's it for me, Mr. Polar Bear. Stay cold out there.

Sincerely,

Greg

Thrones at 38,000 Feet

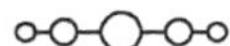

With the axeman storming down the aisle dressed in tarnished medieval armor and shouting for everyone to sit down and be quiet, I ducked behind the seat in front of me. Having just woken from a short in-flight nap, I'd been expecting the drink cart or small snacks, but this was something else altogether.

"I claim this flight and all onboard for the house Targaryen," declared the scar-faced marauder. "All will bow before Khaleesi, the mother of dragons, or feel the swift, unmerciful wrath of my Valyrian steel."

He lifted the heavy axe above his head, which wasn't such an easy thing to do in the tight confines of the Boeing 787 Dreamliner, and lopped off the head of a nearby flight attendant.

"Sit down," the axeman shouted, his booming voice rising above the din of the horrified passengers. "Sit down or you'll be next."

As the screams hushed to terrified whimpers, I peeked over the rows in front of me. The curtain was drawn so I couldn't see what was happening in other parts of the plane, but it seemed fair to assume that a similar madness was occurring throughout the aircraft.

The axeman made threatening grunts and gestures at anyone who so much as glanced in his direction. If there was any doubt about whether he could handle himself, the barbarian put it to rest when three burly men rushed toward him from the Economy Plus section.

Dropping his axe, the skilled warrior drew two short knives from his belt. And, with a sudden flick of his wrists, he let the daggers fly. The first blade found a home in the lead attacker's valiant-but-oh-so-foolish heart, stopping him in his tracks. The second knife, flung a split second after the first, sliced the next attacker's jugular. He, too, fell to the floor like a sack of stale pretzels.

The third attacker stopped to take stock of the situation now that he was alone in this ill-conceived assault. Perhaps he was contemplating a swift retreat. Or maybe his confidence was lifted seeing that the axeman was now unarmed, having left his axe on the floor and used up his daggers. In any event, after this momentary pause, the third attacker charged forward with an earsplitting war-cry to engage the axeman *mano-a-mano*.

As they clinched in mortal combat, that line from *King Lear* popped into my head – the one about how the gods kill us for sport – for that's what it looked like when the axeman gripped the would-be hero's head in his massive metalclad mitts and crushed it like an overripe cantaloupe.

"Enough," commanded the axeman, "Enough of this foolishness."

Throughout the cabin, I watched as the heads of the passengers sank below the tops of the headrests, like a field of prairie dogs slinking back into their holes. Just then, two chimes sounded and the seatbelt sign illuminated.

"Good morning, ladies and gentlemen," said the voice over the intercom. "Greetings from the flight deck. At this time, we're making our final descent into San Francisco. We do expect heavy turbulence for the duration of our flight, so we'll ask everyone, including the cabin crew, to take their seats. Flight attendants, prepare for landing."

"Shut your filthy pie hole," said the axeman, mistaking the voice over the intercom for someone speaking in our section of the plane. His anger enflamed, the burly killer was nevertheless a man accustomed to following commands, as he demonstrated by sitting in an empty seat and fastening his seatbelt.

As I wondered what would happen next, something caught my eye in the opposite aisle. It might have been a child or perhaps someone crawling on all fours. Or maybe it was another foolhardy passenger preparing to make a run at the axeman. Whoever or whatever it was disappeared into the rear galley before I could get a good look.

When the turbulence hit, I shut my eyes and clenched the armrests. Passengers screamed. Metal groaned. And the contents in the overhead bins shifted loudly with each bump and dip. Oh god, I thought, please don't let me die like this, although part of me wondered if it might not be better than whatever fate our captor had in store for us. It seemed to go on like this for an eternity, but the turbulence eventually subsided. And when I opened my eyes, I was surprised to see a stranger sitting in my row (which I'd been lucky enough to have to myself until now). I knew then that it wasn't a child or someone on all fours who'd been scurrying down the aisle. Instead, it was a dwarf, though not just any dwarf – it was Tyrion Lannister from *Game of Thrones*.

I stared in disbelief at the little man.

"If you're not going to finish that," said Tyrion, scooching into the empty middle seat between us and reaching for the small bottle of Chianti I'd tucked into my seat pocket. He twisted open the screw top and guzzled the wine. "We'll be landing soon," he said. "And I for one can't wait to get back on solid ground."

I must have looked like I'd seen a ghost.

"Why so stunned?" asked Tyrion. "You just binge-watched the entire fifth season of *Game of Thrones* on this trans-Atlantic flight. That type of behavior is bound to damage your brain in some way, don't you think?"

I shook my head, as if I could shake some sense into what I was seeing. What the hell's going on here? I wondered. I turned to stare out the window, hoping that by averting my eyes and ignoring his presence the little man would soon disappear. When I looked back, however, Tyrion was still next to me and he was now cradling a wicker basket full of the little wine bottles.

"That's more like it," said the dwarf after downing two bottles in rapid succession, "though I really don't see the point of such small serving sizes."

I wanted to scream. I wanted to run. I wanted to hide from these strange characters come to life on my flight. Then, remembering that the axeman was still buckled into his seat, I wondered if this might be a good time for me to attack him, as if a heroic display of valor on my part might inspire others. Contemplating the likely outcome of such a maneuver, I had a clear vision of my detached head rolling down the aisle like a lopsided bowling ball.

"Have some," said Tyrion, holding out a bottle. "It'll steady your nerves."

Reeling with doubt about the fragile state of my mind, I speculated that this must be what madness looks like and wondered if this was simply a temporary state or if I'd permanently crossed the border into the realm of sheer lunacy. Either way, it dawned on me that I didn't have much to lose at this point.

"That's right," said Tyrion Lannister, as if reading my thoughts. "A little drink never hurt anyone."

"Thank you," I said, reaching for two bottles. "Let's make it a double."

Bad Hombres

Four players from out of town were huddled around the blackjack table getting ready for the dealer to lay down the next cards.

"Hit me," said Bigly. It didn't matter to him that he had 17. He always went for it.

The dealer placed a three of spades on the green felt table.

"I'm good," said Bigly, even though it pained him not to get 21.

"I'm good too," echoed Puppet. It didn't seem to register in his brain that he only had a five of diamonds and a two of hearts. "I'm good," he repeated, staying on seven.

Suspense peeked down at the cards he held close to his vest. "I'm not ready to tell you what I'm going to do," he said.

"That's because you don't have anything," blurted Nasty, who chortled and then uncorked a Texas-sized belch.

"You're a real piece of work, Nasty," said Bigly. "If you're through, let's get back to the game. I have better things I could be doing."

"I'll tell you when I'm through," snapped Nasty, straining his face and letting out a noisome fart. "Why do they call you Bigly anyway? Is it because of the bigly turd in your trousers?"

"Puu-lease," pleaded Suspense. "It's still my turn, and I'm trying to concentrate."

Nasty shot him a look of pure disdain, a look that said, "I'm going to bite off your head and spit it out if you don't hurry up."

"Come on, Suspense," nudged Bigly. "We don't have forever."

"Yeah," repeated Puppet. "We don't have forever."

"Gentlemen, please," said the dealer. "Let's keep it civil."

"You can take your civility and shove it up your ass," said Nasty.

All four players laughed.

"It's to you," said the dealer, ignoring Nasty's rude remark and motioning toward Suspense.

"Oh, I just don't know," he said. "I think I'll make you all wait a little longer."

"Can we get this over with?" asked Bigly. "I have some important business to take care of with a little lady down at the laundromat."

"Loser," smirked Nasty. "You don't have anything going on anywhere."

"Okay, okay," announced Suspense. "I'll stay!"

"Me too," said Puppet, forgetting his turn was already over.

"Hit me, bee-atch," squealed Nasty before the dealer could ask him if he wanted a card or not.

It was seven of clubs to bring Nasty's hand up to nineteen.

"I'm staying!" He belched for good measure.

"Alright, gentlemen," said the dealer. He was lanky, good-looking man named Slash. He laid down his cards to show a six of spades and a four of clubs. "The dealer has ten," he said before placing a card face up on the table. It was the three of clubs.

"Oh, yeah!" roared Bigly. "You're going to bust right now. I can feel it in my bones."

"Me too," squeaked Puppet. "My bones feel it."

"Come on, Mr. Dealer Man," chided Nasty. "Show us a face card so we can walk out of here with all that cash."

"Oh my," said Suspense, fanning his face with a napkin. "This is killing me."

"The dealer has 13," said Slash before turning over his next card.

"Shit," said Bigly and Puppet at nearly the same time.

"The game is rigged," screamed Nasty.

"Sorry, fellas," said Slash, reaching out with his long arms to gather all the chips after laying down the eight of hearts on the table. "But that's how the cookie crumbles sometimes. The dealer has 21."

The locals who were watching the game had big smiles on their faces. They all knew better than to sit at Slash's table. When it came to blackjack, he was the baddest hombre.

Hey, Diddle, Diddle

"Hey, diddle, diddle."

"What are you talking about now?"

"It's the old nursery rhyme. You remember it, right? Hey, diddle, diddle. The cat and the fiddle."

"Don't talk to me about stupid fucking nursery rhymes."

"Hey, diddle, diddle. The cat and the fiddle. The cow jumped over the moon. What do you think it means?"

"It doesn't mean shit, man. Let's get this day started."

"Really, I want to know what you think."

"I just told you what I think. It's a bunch of crap."

"Okay, then, I guess someone woke up on the wrong side of the bed this morning."

"Bed? Wouldn't that be nice. Sounds like one of your bullshit nursery rhymes."

"It's just an expression, Doc. Just a way of saying someone is so cranky they must have gotten up on the wrong side of the bed."

"Whatever."

"Come to think of it, you seem to wake up on the wrong side of bed every morning."

"Now you're starting to get on my nerves, Rico."

"Hey, diddle, diddle."

"Shut up."

"The cat and the fiddle."

"I said shut the fuck up."

"The cow jumped over the moo-oon."

"I'm going to kick your scraggly ass all the way down Market Street."

"Let's do it, Captain Cranky Pants."

"I'm ready whenever you are."

"Right now?"

"Um … let's get breakfast first."

"Breakfast? You holding out me?"

"No, you dipshit, I mean after we get out there and collect

a few bucks for a couple of donuts and some coffee.”

“I get it. So, you’re going to kick my scraggly ass after we hustle some money.”

“That’s right, after I get something in my belly. Are you ready yet?”

“Just a minute. I need to finish my sign. Have you seen the pen?”

“It’s probably up your ass. Hurry it up or we’ll miss the commute traffic.”

“I’m going as fast as I can. Is this how you spell ‘hungery?’”

“Close enough. Let’s get moving ‘cause as my granddad used to say, ‘we’re burning daylight.’”

“I’m coming.”

“Good. Anything else you want to say before we get started?”

“The little dog laughed to see such a sport, and the dish ran away with the spoon.”

A Cure for Writer's Block

Trippy slammed his laptop shut and hurled it against the wall.

The two cats didn't move. Mischief, the asthmatic Siamese, opened his one good eye before falling back asleep. Hemingway, the fat tabby, didn't flinch. She'd been on the losing end of another backyard brawl, a two-inch gash on her forehead still oozing.

Always a prolific writer, Trippy didn't know what to make of his troubling new condition. It had been nearly two months since he'd written a thing. The minute he sat down at his computer his fingers remained frozen above the keyboard as if they'd lost all connection to the brain, and the longer he stared at the screen, the whiter it got – like a snowstorm.

He tried drinking. It made him sick. He tried smoking pot. It made him stare at the cats. He tried taking long walks near the burnt-out pier, but that only managed to get him mugged twice in four days. And when he googled "writer's block" on his new laptop, he quickly came to curse the know-it-alls who claimed to know all about him.

"Crackpots," spat Trippy at the monitor.

He stopped himself from throwing his new laptop, but instead chucked a solid glass paperweight at the wall, where it left a softball-sized indentation, dropped to the floor, and split into pieces. Mischief hissed. Hemingway growled. And Trippy set out for another long walk along the burnt-out pier. At least he didn't get mugged this time.

After two more months of staring at the blank screen, Trippy wondered if he'd ever write again.

"I'm sorry, cats," he said. "Writing's been my life, and you guys have been with me every step of the way. But it might all be over now. I'm stuck."

Both cats lifted their heads and eyeballed Trippy from the opposite side of the room. Mischief got up first, stretching his front left paw, then the right, before limping over and climbing into Trippy's lap. Hemingway meowed and walked the other way, glancing back once before shimmying through the cat door.

"I don't blame you," said Trippy. "Who wants to hang out with a loser?"

Trippy fell asleep on the couch while listening to Mischief's congested wheeze.

When he awoke the next morning, Trippy saw that Hemingway still hadn't returned. It wasn't odd for the cat to stay out late, getting into who-knows-what kind of trouble, but she always made it home in time for breakfast.

Where's that old tabby run off to? thought Trippy.

He rose from the couch and was halfway out the door when Mischief made a small sputtering sound, something between a meow and a cough.

"Wait right there," said Trippy. "I'll be back soon."

He'd only walked a short distance when he spied the marmalade-colored lump in the middle of the road. Hemingway, the grizzled tabby with more than nine lives, had finally run out of luck.

Tears streamed down Trippy's cheeks as he carried the cat's body into the yard. Mischief and Hemingway had been with him from the beginning, since his first published stories, his first novel, and all the rest.

Later that night, after burying Hemingway in the backyard, Trippy returned to the garage to fetch his portable typewriter. He'd seen the light-green Hermes Rocket earlier that day when looking for a shovel. Holding the old typewriter again took him back to those heady times when he wrote for hours on end, often while the two kittens tore through his apartment like a pair of Tasmanian devils.

Trippy blew the dust off the typewriter and carried it back to his desk. A daddy longlegs crawled out from the space between the "Z" and the "X." Otherwise, the old machine looked to be in good shape. He spun a fresh sheet of paper into the carriage and loosened his fingers like a concert pianist about to embark on the performance of a lifetime. His knuckles cracked. His mind focused. Trippy was ready to roll.

He started slowly at first. But Trippy was soon typing at full speed, the unblocked rhythm of the keys pulsing to life under the weight of his eager fingertips as he composed a long and loving tribute to his dear old cat.

The Forest of Red Doors

"I'm looking for a blue door," said the middle-aged woman with cropped white hair.

"Sorry ma'am," replied the security guard dressed in a dark-green uniform. It was his job to man the outpost near the river. "I've only ever seen red doors in the forest."

"Are you sure?" asked the woman, obviously taken aback by the man's words. "I was told to come here to find a blue door."

"I've been stationed in this forest a long time," said the guard. "I'm quite certain there aren't any blue doors here."

"Well," said the woman, "I might as well look around since I'm already here."

As she explored the forest, the woman came upon one red door after another. She found red doors under rocks, behind bushes and trees, and even down by the river. The woman eventually returned to the outpost.

"Well, you're right," she said, slightly out of breath from all the walking. "I must have misunderstood the directions."

"That's alright, ma'am," replied the guard, handing the woman a cup of water. "At least you had a chance to stroll through the forest."

"It's a lovely spot," said the woman. "Thank you for your kindness." She drank the water, handed back the empty cup, and turned to leave.

"Just a moment," said the guard. "Before you go, can you tell me why you're looking for a blue door? Can't you use one of the red doors? They all lead to the same place, right?"

She thought for a moment about how she could explain to this man the dire importance of the blue doors when a small, black bird dropped down from the trees and landed on the guard's left shoulder. The woman and the guard both laughed at such an unexpected intrusion.

"Go to the cave of blue doors," said the bird in a soft, clear voice.

"Excuse me," said the woman, cupping her hand over her ear and leaning in to hear the bird. "What did you say?"

"Go to the cave of blue doors," the bird repeated.

"What are you talking about?" asked the guard. "There's no such a cave in this forest."

"You're wrong," said the bird, who pecked at the man's coat before continuing. "You'll find it at the base of the silver mountain, behind the ancient aspen grove."

With that, the bird took off and flew back into the trees.

"Do you know where we can find the ancient aspens?" asked the woman.

The man lowered his eyes and spoke quietly. "Those trees were cut down last year to make way for a new road."

"Oh no," said the woman, "can you show me where the grove used to be?"

"It won't make any difference," replied the guard.

"Why not?" asked the woman.

"I was in that cave," said the guard. "There weren't any blue doors in there, not that I saw anyway. It was …"

"Take me there right now," demanded the woman.

"As I was saying," continued the guard, "after looking through the cave, we deemed it unsafe."

"Unsafe?" gasped the woman. "What does that mean?"

"It was dangerous," answered the guard. "There were gaping cracks in the floor and loose boulders everywhere. We didn't want anyone to get hurt in the cave so we dynamited the entrance to seal it off."

"You sealed it off?" exclaimed the woman.

"If there were any blue doors in that cave," said the guard, turning to walk back to his outpost, "you'll never get to them now. They're buried under tons of rock."

Follow the Sun to My House of Shells

"Follow the sun to my house of shells," said the hummingbird to the man sitting alone in his car. And with that the hummingbird was gone. Like the barely remembered thread of a rich and vivid dream.

The man wiped the sleep from his eyes and yawned to greet the morning. He was waiting for something, though if you asked him what he wouldn't have been able to tell you. He looked down at the half-eaten donut on the passenger seat and then cast his glance toward the bushes near the car for places where a hummingbird might hide.

"What's the house of shells," whispered the man, "and how can I follow the sun to get there?"

It was dark outside, but the neighborhood was waking up. A handful of people had already walked by. A woman dressed in bright orange and purple sweats swept the sidewalk in front of a pet grooming salon. Meanwhile, on the other side of the street, a homeless man gesticulated oratorically as if lecturing to a hall packed with eager students, except that there wasn't anyone on the street to hear him. A filthy sleeping bag was draped over his shoulder like the toga on some kind of modern-day philosopher. A Stoic perhaps, thought the man, recalling something he'd heard long ago in an undergraduate philosophy course.

The man bit into his half-eaten donut. It's not too stale, he thought, and took another bite. He watched himself in the rearview mirror, chewing. When he finished the donut, the man licked the sugar off his fingertips and brushed the crumbs from his shirt. He looked out the windshield then and noticed the early-morning rays of the sun shining brightly off the corrugated metal rooftop of the shuttered warehouse across the street.

With that, the man sat up in the driver's seat. He gripped the steering wheel with his left hand, while reaching forward with his right to turn the key in the ignition.

"Here we go," said the man. "Now I can follow the sun to the house of shells."

His newfound enthusiasm was matched just as suddenly – and just strongly – by an overwhelming wave of sadness as the hollow clickety-clickety-clack of the car's dead engine reminded the man that he wasn't going anywhere.

A Day Off

Sam sits on his patio reading a book. It's a quiet day, a great day for doing nothing but relaxing with a good book, which is all Sam wants to do. This is his first day off work in more than a year.

The doorbell rings.

Sam: Crap.

He ignores the bell. It rings again.

Sam: Crap, crap, crap.

He shuts the book, puts it down, and goes to open the door. It's his boss, Sally.

Sam: Sally? What are you doing here?

She rushes in, removes her coat, and throws it on a chair.

Sam:	What's going on? I was just about to read, but come on in.

Sally:	Don't worry, this won't take long, but I need to ask you something.

Sam:	It couldn't wait until tomorrow at work?

Sally walks out to the patio, sits on Sam's couch, and picks up his book. She skims through the pages distractedly and tosses the book on the couch. It bounces off a cushion and lands on the floor.

Sally:	Do you have anything to drink? A glass of water perhaps? (Sam starts to move.) No, lemonade. (Sam stops, looks at her, and takes another step.) No, Diet Coke. (Sam stops again.) No, bourbon!

After waiting to see if Sally's going to change her mind again, Sam goes to the kitchen and returns a few minutes later with the drink.

Sam:	Okay, here you go … bourbon … neat! That's how you like it, right? (Under his breath, he adds…) At ten o'clock in the morning.

She chugs the entire glass full of bourbon in one gulp.

Sally:	Perfect!

Sam looks at Sally, waiting for her to say whatever she's come to say.

Sally: So, Sam, you're probably wondering why
               I'm here …

Sam opens his mouth to say something, but Sally cuts him off.

Sally: I just wanted to come by to tell you
               something … (she pauses) … something
               very important.

Sam listens.

Sally: You see, Sam, ever since we began
               working together, I … I … I …

The doorbell rings before she completes her sentence. Sam turns to get the door, but Sally reaches out to grab him.

Sally: Don't get it, honey!

Sam: Honey? (Taken aback, Sam moves away.)

Sally: I meant to say …

The doorbell rings again.

Sam: I'll be back in a second.

When Sam leaves the room, Sally reaches into her purse for a cigarette and lights it. Sam returns to the patio with a panicked look on his face.

Sam: What's this all about?

He's followed by a large man holding a pistol. It's George, Sally's husband.

Sally:	George!
George:	Shut up, both of you. I finally caught you in the act with this slimeball.
Sam:	What?
Sally:	I'm so sorry, honey.

George and Sam (at the same time): Honey?

Sally:	I was going to tell you, Sam, but I didn't have a chance.
Sam:	Tell me what?
George:	Yeah, tell him what?
Sally:	I love you, Sam.
Sam:	What?
George:	I knew it!
Sam:	Wait a minute here.
Sally:	I've loved you since the day you came to work for us. Remember how it rained cats and dogs that day?
Sam:	Um, no.
Sally:	Anyway, that's why I never gave you a day off. Because I wanted to be near you all day, every day.
George:	I knew you two were up to something.

Sam: Listen, George, I don't know what's going on here.

Sally: Oh, Sam.

Sally rushes over and kisses Sam on the lips. He pushes Sally away. She trips over a chair and bumps her head on the couch. She's not hurt from the fall, but she's sobbing.

Sam: Get away from me. You're crazy! You're both crazy! (He points at George) And put down that gun before someone gets hurt.

George: (Puts his gun on the table and moves toward Sally.) Are you okay, princess?

Sally: (Rubbing the back of her head.) Oh, George. I'm so sorry. I don't know what got over me. (She looks at Sam.) What are you doing here?

Sam: Me? What are you talking about? This is my apartment.

She stands up and hugs her husband.

Sally: Well then, I don't know what we're doing here. (She looks at George.) Let's go home, sweetie. (She continues to rub her head.) Jeez, this is some kind of headache.

George looks at Sam and shrugs. He holds Sally tighter.

George: I'd better get you home, darling. (He
                    picks up his gun and waves it at Sam.)
                    You're lucky I'm a forgiving person.

George and Sally leave arm in arm. The door shuts behind
them.

Sam: Lunatics! (He says it quietly, not wanting
                    George to hear him and return.)

Sam bolts the door, then goes into the kitchen. When he
comes back, he's holding a glass filled with bourbon. He
drinks it down in one gulp, sits on the couch, and picks up
his book.

Sam: Okay then, what page was I on?

The Long Path

Max marched down the leaf-covered path, his heavy footsteps leaving a trail of soggy impressions in the mud. A chainsaw growled in the distance. And a pair of crows screeched at each other with violent intent, causing Max to pause for a few beats before continuing on his way. Pacing off his steps like he was following an ancient treasure map, Max stopped at three mossy boulders, turned to look back up the path to make sure he wasn't being followed, and veered off into the trees. I'm almost there, he thought, shifting his shovel to the opposite shoulder.

A noise in the forest stopped Max in his tracks. Not wanting to take any chances, he ducked behind a tree and reached for the Colt .45 tucked into the back of his jeans.

"Who's there?" he called out.

No one answered.

Wiping the sweat off his forehead with the back of his arm, Max was ready to move on when a staccato burst shattered the quiet of the forest. His nerves already jangled, Max nearly fired off a shot into the canopy.

"Stupid woodpecker!" he hissed, his heart beating hard in his chest.

Max tucked the gun into his waistband and kept walking. It wasn't long before he heard what sounded like muffled footsteps. No doubt about it, he thought, I'm being followed.

Max tossed the shovel to the side, spun quickly, and pointed his gun.

"Alright," he said. "Come out. I know you're there."

Max held the gun steady, ready for whoever was stalking him.

"Nice and easy. I'm not afraid to use this thing."

When his pursuer stepped into the open, Max couldn't help but laugh. He was being followed by the old goat he'd passed at the top of the path.

"You son-of-a-bitch," said Max. "I should shoot you right now for scaring the crap out of me."

The goat lowered its head to munch on a patch of weeds.

Max kicked a pinecone in the animal's direction and

walked on. The only thing he heard now was the sucking sound of his boots sticking in the mud.

It had been seven years since Max had last been in these woods. Seven years of waiting for the day he could reclaim what they'd left behind.

From the moment of his arrest, Max had stuck to his story that Johnny had been the brains behind the job. Johnny had a long rap sheet and a reputation among local law enforcement for being a two-bit ring leader of this type of two-bit operation. It also didn't hurt Max's case that this had been his first arrest. It made it easier for him to convince the cops, the judge, and anyone else who paid attention that he'd been played by Johnny all along. Max got seven years, but it could have been worse.

Walking deeper into the forest, Max's eyes lit up when he spied the charred stump. On his imaginary treasure map, this was where "X" marked the spot. Max peeled off his windbreaker and pushed the shovel into the soggy ground.

His story hadn't been a complete fabrication. It had been Johnny's idea to rob the bank and hide the money in the forest. It had also been Johnny's intention to double-cross Max and grab the cash for himself. Whether it had been beginner's luck or his paranoia kicking into overdrive, Max had sniffed out his partner's treachery. And in that instant when Johnny made his move, Max was ready.

The shovel nudged up against something hard. If Max didn't know any better, he might have thought it was a large rock or a root from the burnt-out stump. He slid the sharp edge of the shovel lower and lifted Johnny's skull out of the ground.

"Long time no see," said Max as he rolled the mud-caked cranium off to the side.

Johnny had it all figured out.

"We'll bury the money in the woods," he'd said. "And wait for the heat to die down."

Max continued digging, pushing the shovel deeper into the ground. He was working faster now, sweat running off his forehead and into his eyes, and he almost didn't notice when the shovel pushed through the thread-bare canvas sack they'd used to carry the money.

Dropping to his knees, Max thrust his hands into the sack, pulled out a clump of mud, and flung it onto the mound he'd created next to the ditch. He plunged his hands further into the sack and pulled out another soggy mess. He was about to add it to the pile when something caught his eye.

"What the …"

Max clawed at the sludge with his hands, and only then did it dawn on him that it wasn't just mud he was removing from the sack. It was also the decomposed remains of what had once been nearly $200,000.

"Seven years," Max shouted. "I've been waiting seven lousy years for this?"

Johnny's plan had been solid in every way, except one.

It had been dry when they buried the sack next to the stump. The entire region had been suffering through severe drought for nearly a decade. After years of dry weather, however, their perfect burial spot had turned into a swampy, soupy quagmire. The cash, if you could still call it that, was nothing more than gunky lumps of greenish-brown pulp.

Max stood, picked up the shovel, and waved it wildly before smashing it down on Johnny's skull. Fragments of bone flew into the air and landed in the mud. Max swung down on the skull again and again and again, continuing until his energy was spent.

"Seven years," he moaned.

When a twig snapped behind him, Max stumbled while reaching for his Colt .45 and accidentally fired a shot straight down into the meat of his leg. Dropping to the ground in pain, his blood gushing uncontrollably from a punctured artery, Max screamed in agony as the old goat appeared from behind a bush to feast on the weeds sprouting all around the secret burial spot.

Breakfast with the Alien

Spiders

Hundreds of mouse-sized spiders were released into the city. Municipal authorities had devised the plan, in coordination with various local, state, and federal agencies, to inject the mouse-spiders with a genetically-modified serum that programmed the hairy black arachnids to hunt down and eradicate the disease carriers once and for all.

In the first and only large-scale test of the mouse-spiders, held in an abandoned shopping mall at the edge of the plague-infested city, scientists created a lab of sorts by placing infected humans and uninfected volunteers in side-by-side rooms. Scientists, politicians, and security personnel watched on a bank of flickering monitors in the control room as the spiders, unleashed like trained attack dogs, crept from room to room.

Given the freedom to come and go as they pleased, would the mouse-spiders do as they were programmed and strike down the infected? Or would they lash out at anything that moved, killing the volunteers and putting an end once and for all to civilization's hope for recovery? That's what was at stake.

The test was going as planned until a particularly large spider entered the room of a healthy volunteer who'd fallen asleep on a sheet of cardboard. Scientists and security forces watched as the eight-legged creature the size of a large fist crawled up onto the volunteer's leg, then onto her blouse, and to within inches of her exposed neck. It halted there for an instant, as if sniffing.

"Wait," whispered the command leader into the security intercom. "Let's give this a few more seconds to play out." Her security forces were ready to rush in with flamethrowers that would incinerate the rogue mouse-spider as well as the sleeping volunteer.

Just as she was about to give the word to proceed, the command leader held her breath for another two-count and watched as the spider backed away.

"Stand down," she breathed into the mic. "Stand down."

Leaving through a carved-out hole in the wall, the spider emerged in the next room where it wasted no time leaping onto the neck of one of the infected and sunk its fangs deep into its fleshy, diseased jugular.

"That was close," said the team leader. "But at least we know it works."

Three days later, she gave the order to unleash the mouse-spiders on the entire city.

Throwing a Turkey

"I want to throw a turkey."

My sister was always saying crazy things like that.

"Go ahead," I said, not looking up from the comic book. "Like I fucking even know what you're talking about."

"Mo-ommmy!" She started running before I could grab her. "Buddy said the F word."

I have to give it to the speedy little runt. Those pipsqueak feet carried her out of my reach before I could even think of getting off the couch. At least she was finally out of my room.

"Buddy, did you say the F word?" my mother asked from the kitchen. "Why can't you be nice to your sister?"

"Because she's a freaking lunatic," I said, but not loud

enough for anyone to hear me.

I went back to turning the pages very carefully on my latest purchase – a mint edition of *Iron Man and Sub-Mariner #1*. I'd finally saved enough money from mowing lawns to buy this "Special Once-in-a-Lifetime Issue."

"But he called me the F word." My sister was still pleading her case.

"I didn't call her anything," I said, which was technically accurate.

"Mo-ommmy," she continued, "you said he'd be in big trouble if he used any more curse words."

Damn, I thought, she's out to get me this time. What's with all that crap about throwing a turkey anyway? Where does she come up with these ridiculous ideas?

"Now, Jenn," I heard my mother say, "No one likes a tattler."

Way to have my back, Mom, I thought, and returned to my comic book. The phone rang in the other room and my sister picked it up.

"Daddy, daddy, daddy," she said, "Buddy called me the F word and made me cry."

She'd learned early on that if you don't succeed with one judge, take your case to another court.

"OK," she said, "I'll tell him. Oh, and I love, love, love you, Daddy." And with that the little kiss-ass took the phone into the kitchen and handed it off to Mom. I couldn't hear what my parents were talking about, but I could guess it had something to do with me and my foul mouth.

As I strained to overhear what my mother was saying, my sister came strutting through the doorway with a big, gloating smile stretched across her face. You'd think she just won an Academy Award.

"I'm trying to read," I said, trying my best to ignore her.

"Daddy said he's going to talk to you tonight about your swearing." She paused just long enough to make sure I didn't pounce. "You're going to be grounded."

She was still on her toes, ready to bolt, but I didn't move a muscle – as much as I wanted to wipe that stupid smirk off her face.

"Hey, Buddy," she said. "Hey, Buddy, did I tell you I was reading a book about bowling?"

I didn't say a word.

"Did you know it's called a turkey when you throw three strikes in a row? Wanna come bowling with me? I want to throw a turkey."

"Me and you bowling?" I said, looking up from *Iron Man and Sub-Mariner #1*. "Are you out of your mind? I'd rather babysit the Blutowski triplets than be seen with you at the bowling alley."

And with that she was running for the kitchen again.

"Mo-ommmy," she said, even louder than before. "Buddy called me the F word again."

The tone of my mother's footsteps changed as she hurried toward my room, her pace quickening as she moved from the kitchen linoleum to the hardwood hallway. I slipped the comic book into its protective sleeve and slid it under the couch. I didn't want anything to damage my new prized possession.

My sister was probably right. I'd be grounded for a few days, whether I deserved it or not. But that's alright, I thought, because in my mind I was already planning an afternoon of bowling with my buddies. And I couldn't wait to see the look on that little whiner's face when I told her all about it, especially the part about how much fun it had been to throw a turkey.

Eros at the Bus Stop

Eros sat on the bench at the dimly lit bus stop, his left wing broken, his quiver empty. The thick glass walls of the bus stop were shattered, the digital bus-tracker read "out of order," and the place reeked of urine. He wasn't there for long when a homeless woman with two missing front teeth came and sat beside him.

"Aren't you cold?" she asked, peeking down at the loose white fabric draped over his loins.

"Come to think of it, I am," replied Eros. "I am cold." It's not a sensation he's ever felt before.

"I'd let you borrow my coat if I had one," said the gap-toothed woman.

"That's sweet of you," said Eros, "but I'll be fine." If not for the layers of caked-on grime and the unkempt hair, she'd be an attractive woman, he thought.

"Do you know when the bus comes?" asked the woman.

"I don't have a clue," said Eros, "I don't normally ride on public transportation." He pointed over his shoulder at the broken wing.

"What happened?"

"I'm not sure," said Eros. "One minute I was dancing in the clouds and shooting arrows like any other day, and then I suddenly fell out of the sky." He rubbed a bruise on his rear. "It gave me quite a jolt."

The homeless woman smiled sweetly and patted his bare thigh. "I guess we all have our bad days," she said.

A loud hacking cough came from the dark doorway across the street. Eros and the homeless woman stared, waiting for whoever it was to make himself known.

"Who's there?" yelled the woman.

"No need to shout," answered a man's raspy voice. "I can hear you just fine, Irma." He leaned out of the shadows to show his dirty, scabrous face.

"Oh, it's Archie," said the woman.

"A friend of yours?" asked Eros.

"I wish," she replied. "He's quite handsome when he's cleaned up." She blushed and turned away.

"Ah ha, I see," said the god of love.

Eros bent forward to pick up his bow. It doesn't seem to be damaged, he thought, testing the tension of the string. Then he reached over his shoulder for an arrow, which made him remember they'd all been lost in the fall.

"I'm sorry I can't be of any help," said Eros.

He rose dejectedly and began to limp away, the feathers on his broken wing dragging on the cold sidewalk.

"Hey, wait a minute," called the woman. "You're going to miss the bus."

Sauerkraut and Grape Jelly

I rolled in at 1:30 AM. Well, rolled in isn't exactly accurate. It was more like two stumbles and a lurch through the doorway. Whatever you want to call it, I got home late and made a beeline for the refrigerator. Somewhere in my brain fog I recalled there being a single can of beer hiding in the back corner, behind the sauerkraut and grape jelly.

How would those two things go together, I wondered? The phone in the living room rang before I could speculate further about that culinary delight.

"Hello," I said, making a conscious effort not to sound groggy.

"Syd?" said the voice on the other end of the line. "Is that you?"

"Yeah," I answered. "Who's this?"

"It's Mort."

"Mort!" I said. "Long time no see. Did we have a good time tonight or what?"

"Yeah, we had a great time until you pulled a disappearing act."

I let those words sink in: "pulled a disappearing act." What was he talking about? Was this one of his practical jokes? Was he confusing me with someone else? Was he smoking too much of that ragweed again? Then it hit me. When Mort went to the bathroom at the club, I slid off my barstool, put on my overcoat, and walked home.

"Oh man," I said. "Are you still at the bar?"

"Yes, I am."

"Crap. I'm sorry, Mort."

"It's okay. I just wanted to make sure you got home in one piece."

After Mort hung up, I stood there staring at the phone, as if it might tell me why I left my friend at the bar. Then I remembered what I was doing in the kitchen in the first place.

"Beer," I said. "Where are you, beer?"

I reached deep into the top shelf, nudging my fingers past jars and bottles and boxes of leftovers, but I couldn't get my hand on the beer can. When I bent down for a closer look, I saw the sauerkraut and the grape jelly right where I thought they'd be, but the beer was gone.

I guess I already finished it off, I thought, grabbing the grape jelly and sauerkraut jars and placing them on the counter. It didn't take long to spread the ingredients evenly on two slices of sourdough.

"You should be here, Morty," I mumbled before biting into the unlikeliest of sandwiches.

Call Me

Amelia paused before calling Sal. She wanted to organize her thoughts before getting him on the phone. She and Sal had been good friends for years, going back to their days as interns at a large corporate law firm in San Francisco, and they continued to stay in touch after going different directions in their careers.

As interns, Sal and Amelia learned early on they had a lot in common. Similar interests. Similar values. And a shared sense of humor. They spent the entire internship working together on the same project – a never-ending asbestos case – and they often went out for long lunches and after-dinner drinks.

They talked about work. They talked about where they were from and where they were going. And they talked about their relationships. In those days, Amelia was living with a fisherman named Rex who, as she later found out, had a plaything in every port. As for Sal, he was engaged to his high school sweetheart, a former cheerleader named DeeDee, who, after undergoing a sex change operation, now goes by Davey.

As the years passed, Sal and Amelia continued to confide in each another about their disastrous relationships, not only with Rex and DeeDee/Davey, but also with a series of subsequent partners. Through all the tough times, they remained close friends who often shared beers and tears, though it never occurred to either of them to sleep together – until last night.

"I don't know about this," Sal had said, as Amelia leaned forward to kiss him.

"Why not?" she asked. "We know everything else about each other. We might as well see what it's like."

"It's not that I don't want to," said Sal, "but I hate the thought of ruining a perfectly good friendship."

"We're adults," replied Amelia. "I think we can handle it."

"What the hell," he said, unbuttoning his shirt.

"That's the spirit," said Amelia.

When she awoke this morning, Amelia saw that Sal was gone. He didn't leave a note, a text, a voice message. Nothing. He'd slipped out like a burglar careful not to leave behind even one fingerprint.

Amelia waited until the evening before calling.

"Hi, Sal," she said into the answering machine. "I'm just checking in to see how you're doing. Maybe we can grab a beer tomorrow … or something." Amelia paused before continuing. "Call me," she said into the phone, though she had a sinking feeling that she wouldn't be talking to Sal again any time soon.

Trump III

The year is 2073. As part of a new effort to curb population growth, President-Emperor Donald J. Trump III, who originally campaigned under the banner of "The Best Trump Ever," has decreed a new law, effective immediately.

Whereas pedestrians have been guaranteed the right of way throughout our great land, let it be known forthwith that this is no longer the case. We now deem it vital to our country's survival for vehicles – of all shapes and sizes – to aim for and without any warning whatsoever run down pedestrians whether they be in or outside the crosswalk, on or off the sidewalk, or exposed in any way, shape, or form. Let this be the law of the land, starting October 2nd, 2073, in this the 56th year of the Trump dynasty.

At first, the public at large didn't know what to make of

such a declaration. Pedestrians, in general, continued to walk the streets freely as if nothing had changed. Drivers, likewise, were hesitant to alter their ways. Over time, however, people began to understand the logic behind Trump's law. "By cutting down the losers," said a government spokesman from the West Wing of the Gold House, "we will make sure there's more food, water, housing, and other resources for the winners."

Civic duty aside, something above and beyond limiting population growth began to appeal to the masses. People – well, drivers anyway – started to appreciate the bloodsport that went hand-in-hand with Trump's decree. In the first days after the law went into effect, the hush of the nuclear-powered vehicles made it easy to pick off jaywalkers and other pedestrians. As people grew more savvy about how they walked the streets, drivers became increasingly creative about how they approached the challenge of population control. They began to outfit their vehicles with spikes, spears, and NRA-distributed machine guns for hunting down even the most cunning of streetwalkers. They also sported special decals on their vehicles to mark their kills – like combat pilots of a bygone era who tracked the number of enemy planes shot down.

A year after the law went into effect, Trump III appeared in a holo-cast from the Gold House to congratulate himself on the initiative's success. "We're winning," he declared triumphantly. "We're winning and now we're going to win some more." With that, he announced an amendment to the law that awarded huge tax breaks to the drivers who took out the most pedestrians.

"What can I say?" said Trump III during his subsequent re-election campaign (in which he was running unopposed for a third consecutive term). "I identified a problem and solved it. Just like I always do. I can't help it if I'm a genius, right?"

With that, our President-Emperor cast his gaze straight into the camera to deliver the final words of his speech: "Stay safe out there my fellow Americans."

The Changeling

"Bring me the infant," said Rael, "quickly and quietly."

Effinia slipped out of the room, quickly and quietly, tiptoeing down the dimly lit hospital corridor. She found the basket where they'd left it tucked under a bundle of linens. When lifting the cover to see that everything was in place, she was greeted by a small gurgling noise that made her smile.

"Quickly and quietly," Effinia remembered as she lifted the basket and hurried back to the room where Rael was waiting.

"Here it is," said Effinia. "Everything is in order."

"'She,'" corrected Rael, "you must learn to say 'here she is.'"

"Forgive me, Commander. The earthling pronouns still confuse me."

With that, Rael hoisted the human baby out of the cradle. The little creature is heavier than she looks, thought Rael, who motioned for Effinia to put the gurgling bundle into the vacated space.

"Are you sure she's programmed to grow at the standard Earth rate?"

"Yes, Rael" answered Effinia. "I double-checked the bio calibration." She paused and then added. "She's beautiful, don't you think?"

"Of course," said Rael. "She's the perfect copy."

When the replica was safely tucked away in the nursery, Rael and Effinia left the room. Without a sound, they crept down the hallway on their clawed feet and marched away from the hospital building.

"What now?" whispered Effinia, holding the basket with the human infant.

"We wait for the mothership," said Rael, scanning the gray night sky, "and then we prepare the feast."

Breakfast with the Alien

Via Negativa

Welcome to the Via Negativa. That's what I say to myself every afternoon when I step behind the bar. To be accurate, I don't "say it" as much as hum it in my head to the tune of "Hotel California."

Welcome to the Via Negativa
Such a lonely place (such a lonely place)
Such a worn-out face
Plenty of room at the Via Negativa
Any time of year (any time of year)
you can find me here

I start my day by walking the length of the counter, making sure everything's in its place and wiping away the sticky remains from last night's spills. Did I leave the place such a mess?

No one's come in yet today, but they'll be here soon enough. The Giants are playing a winner-take-all playoff game tonight against the Mets. Madbum's pitching and it's Orange October. That's sure to draw a crowd.

Two guys in suits come in and order beers.

"Go Giants," says one of them, slapping down a healthy tip on the countertop. It's a good omen to start the day.

I pour myself a shot and go back to making sure the place is ready for tonight.

Another guy walks in without saying a word and heads to the back wall where he stops to stare up at the television.

"What's it going to be, Captain Emptyhands?" I ask.

I don't mind people hanging out at the bar. But they need to order at least one drink. We have some guys who crawl in when the door opens and nurse a drink for hours. Others crack open their laptop and work here all day. It's all good as far as I'm concerned, so long as they buy something – and leave the appropriate tip, of course.

Freddy Freeloader turns and leaves without speaking a word.

"Keep walking, loser," I mumble.

The two suits stop their conversation and give me that you-talking-to-me glare.

"Not you guys," I assure them. "What are you having? This round's on me."

"Now you're talking," says one of the businessmen. "I'll have a shot of tequila."

"Make it two," says his partner.

"You got it, boys. And I'm going to join you, if you don't mind."

I pour three short glasses of *anejo*.

"Go Giants," we all say, knocking our glasses together.

That should keep me going for a few hours, I think.

The three Mexican drywallers from the remodel across the street saunter into the bar for their regular drink after work. It's three o'clock and they've already put in more than a full day by the look of their overalls and the dust in their hair.

"Hola, amigos," I call out.

"Hola, gringo," one of them replies.

We share a good laugh, and they order tequila.

"And one for you, too, *viejo*," says one of the workers.

"Vamos Gigantes!" we say, clinking glasses.

I walk down to the end of the bar humming to myself. *Welcome to the Via Negativa.* Like it says in the song, "you can check out any time you like but you can never leave." They got that line right, I think while pouring myself another shot.

The Guitarist in the Doorway

The guitarist liked to play in different spots throughout the neighborhood. In recent weeks, he'd set up in the doorway of an abandoned building that used to be a hair salon. The Vietnamese woman who ran the business packed up and moved not too long ago, as did the other nearby shop owners, when an out-of-town developer received the go-ahead to break ground on a new condo complex that would dwarf all other buildings in the area.

I don't know if the guitarist ever fully grasped what was going on with the new development. There were signs posted explaining the next steps, but I doubt he paid any attention to them. The one time I spoke to him, he felt threatened and lifted his guitar as if to smash it over my head if I stepped any closer.

"Okay, okay," I said. "Take it easy, buddy. I didn't mean any harm."

He didn't say a word. He just sat down and continued playing as I moved away.

I kept my distance after that, though I'd watch him from the opposite side of the street as I waited for the bus. One day I noticed his guitar was held together with haphazard strips of blue tape, as if it had a deep wound stitched up by an unskilled surgeon. Maybe someone got too close, I thought, and the guitar player let them have it with his old acoustic.

The guitarist never sang, though you could sometimes hear him humming. He wasn't the world's greatest player, but he wasn't terrible either. He played a lot, that's for sure, often practicing his scales by walking his fingers up and down the fretboard as if his life depended on it.

I don't know where the guitarist spent the night. Maybe he plopped down wherever he could find a spot. In an alleyway. Behind a bush. Under the freeway overpass. Maybe he stayed at the shelter by the freeway onramp. Or maybe he lived in one of those tents by the railroad crossing. I'd seen him over there every now and then, walking alongside the tracks like he might catch a southbound freighter. Like a hobo who rides the rails from city to city in search of a job, a meal, a fresh start.

Whenever he finished playing for the day, the guitarist would sling his guitar over his shoulder and shuffle off to who-knows-where. He also carried a military-style duffle bag. Maybe he had a change of clothes in the bag, though from what I'd seen he wore the same things every day. Clay-red pants, ripped and frayed. A faded gray t-shirt. And a dark blue Derby jacket, like the kind I used to wear in high school.

The last time I saw the guitarist was the morning when construction crews began tearing down the building next to the hair salon. He was in particularly good form that day, and I even thought about crossing the street to tell him how good he sounded. Then I remembered the last time I tried to talk to him. No, I thought, I'll stay right where I am. Before boarding the bus, I looked back one last time to see him playing, blissfully unaware as a pair of backhoes clawed away at the structures around him.

I read later in our local newspaper that he was chased off by the construction foreman, but the details are murky after that. Some say he misjudged the angle when trying to hop on the train. Others speculate that he was simply crossing the tracks at the wrong time and never knew what hit him.

Another story that began circulating was told by an old homeless man who said he saw the guitarist walk onto the tracks.

"He lifted his guitar like so," said the old man, raising his arms like a slugger at the plate.

In my mind, I could picture exactly what happened next when, as the homeless man told it, the guitarist stepped forward and swung with all his might, as if he could stop the oncoming train with one wild swing of his patched-up old guitar.

Speechless

Mrs. Snoodgrass wasn't speechless very often. She had what folks in these parts call "the gift of gab." So, anytime she stopped talking for more than a few seconds, you were bound to take notice.

Her full name was Henrietta J. Snoodgrass (Henny to her friends). No one knew where she came from, and no one knew exactly how she amassed such a considerable fortune. Still, everyone in the community admired Mrs. Snoodgrass for her generosity to a multitude of charitable endeavors, especially when it came to funding for the Arts.

On the day in question, Mrs. Snoodgrass and a gaggle of city figures and socialites had come together in the city's renowned arts district to break ground on a state-of-the-art symphony hall that would from this day forward bear the name of its esteemed benefactress. It was during this ceremony that Mrs. Snoodgrass, not to mention everyone else in attendance, was rendered speechless.

What caused this most unusual state of affairs? How, in other words, did Mrs. Snoodgrass lose her gift of gab? Rest assured, dear reader, I'll get to that in good time. Suffice it to say that the day began in splendid fashion. There was nary a cloud in the sky as the Littleton High School marching band kicked off the activities by parading on the space dedicated to the new concert hall. After that, Mayor Spittlebury and other dignitaries praised Mrs. Snoodgrass for her enduring generosity.

"Hers is a legacy that shall live on forever," declared the mayor.

All the fine words and pageantry led up to the day's big event, the ceremonial ground-breaking. Just as the mayor was about to kick the gold-plated shovel into the dirt, he and everyone else who was gathered around were distracted by the most unusual sight of Sheriff Humperdinck and four of his finest deputies, in a noticeable state of excitement, running their way.

"Whatever is the cause for such alarm?" exclaimed Mrs. Snoodgrass.

"Don't you worry, Henny," assured the mayor. "Let's just wait a minute for them to pass through, then we'll continue with the festivities."

Indeed, Mayor Spittlebury, Mrs. Snoodgrass, and everyone else expected the sheriff and his men to run past the gathering to take care of their police business. Instead the officers came to a heavy-booted stop in the middle of the crowd.

"Oh my goodness," cried Mrs. Snoodgrass. "What's the meaning of this intrusion, Ralph? Surely, this can wait until after the ceremony?"

"I'm afraid not, ma'am," replied Sheriff Humperdinck, who was noticeably short of breath from his sprint up Main Street, and not a little bit red-faced for having to interrupt the proceedings. Nevertheless, the lawman had his duty to fulfill.

"I'm sorry to say, Mrs. Snoodgrass," continued the sheriff, still catching his breath, "that it's my unpleasant task to inform you of a warrant for your arrest."

Pulling an official-looking paper from his vest pocket, Sheriff Humperdinck proceeded to read the warrant against Mrs. Henrietta J. Snoodgrass, sharing the sordid details of how the wealthy socialite had come by her fortune through deeds most nefarious.

Long ago, so the warrant would have us believe, Mrs. Snoodgrass, under the name of Veronica Sidebottom, had married a reclusive banking tycoon named Elroy Lagrange. According to the warrant, Mrs. Snoodgrass (Henny of all people!) murdered old-man Lagrange on their wedding night by puncturing his heart with a sterling silver icepick. The bride, it seems, had plotted all along not only to murder her new husband, but also to high-tail it out of town with six crates of gold bars the banker hid away in his mansion (seeing that he didn't put an ounce of trust in his very own bank or any other to keep his money safe).

Certain information had come to light recently, said the sheriff as he folded the warrant and returned it to his vest, that Mrs. Snoodgrass was indeed Veronica Sidebottom, the fugitive bride.

As Sheriff Humperdinck handcuffed the newly dishonored benefactress, two of her dearest friends, Mrs. Bigly and the hunchbacked widow Breckinridge, fainted on the spot where the mayor had only minutes beforehand rested the gold-plated shovel. While the mayor and others attended to the stricken ladies, Mrs. Olivander, another one of Henny's closest friends, fanned herself wildly and asked no one in particular, "Whatever will we call the new symphony hall now?"

Woke Up This Morning

I woke up drenched in sweat, my t-shirt and boxer shorts soaked through and sticking to my body like an extra layer of skin. It didn't matter that I'd kept the old ceiling fan going all night. Wop-wop-wobbly-wop. Like a helicopter in distress. I'd kept the sliding glass door open, too, while covering myself with the thinnest of sheets. Just something to lay over my body like a flimsy security blanket, something to protect me from the mosquitoes.

This season of record-breaking heat left me feeling lethargic, irritable, and downright miserable, but it didn't bother me as much as the mosquitoes. They drove me crazy, with their incessant whine getting louder and louder in my half-sleep until it seemed like they were dive-bombing me in surround sound. I'd wave my arm or pillow or draw my thin sheet over my face, but nothing deterred

the little kamikazes from strafing my ears while looking for
a fleshy landing spot.

Last night, when I was sure I wouldn't get any sleep at all
if I didn't stop the onslaught, I pulled the sheet over my
chest and waited, thinking that if I remained still I could
lure the persistent blood-sucker into a trap. I'd be the
bait, aiming to turn from hunted to hunter at just the right
moment. Closer and closer it came until …

I slapped my palm against my cheek. "Got you, you little
shit."

I switched on the bedside lamp and reached for my glasses.
The crushed, mushy, blood-red remains of my nemesis
lay squarely in the center of my hand. Breathing a sigh of
relief, I wiped what was left of the spindly-legged bug on
the side of my mattress and rolled over to get some sleep –
finally.

As I dozed off, lulled toward the land of dreams by the
droning wop-wop-wobbly-wop of the dysfunctional fan,
I heard a faint though unmistakable whine. It can't be, I
thought. But it was! In my moment of victory, after finally
slaying the beast, I'd neglected to account for the fact that
there might be more than one mosquito in the room.

But how are they getting in, I wondered? It couldn't be
the screen door. I'd recently replaced the old screen, the
one with gashes so large a squadron of mosquitoes could
have flown through it in formation. Were they squeezing
through the mesh holes? Or could they stealthily slide
open the door like cat burglars while I slept? Regardless

of how the mosquitoes got in, I knew the blame for this mess ultimately fell on the shoulders of my neighbors, the bastards with the moss-covered koi pond in their unkempt and overgrown backyard.

I kept hoping the neighbors would move. Or at least have the common sense to empty the pond when word began spreading about the new and more virulent strain of Zika. When neither of those things happened, I thought about sneaking over the fence and poisoning the fish. Maybe that would lead them to remove the stagnant water. That's about the time, however, when the heatwave hit and the fish began dying off on their own. I'd peek out my bedroom window and see their bloated orange and white bodies floating on the surface. What a way to die, I thought, boiled in your own koi pond. Well, at least I wouldn't have to kill the fish.

Wop-wop-wobbly-wop. The fan continued to spin as the mosquito buzzed near my ear. I yanked the threadbare sheet over my head and contemplated my next strategy.

Furious George

You've probably heard of my cousin Curious George. Well, he's my second cousin really, but who's counting. In any event, he refuses to have anything to do with me since that night a few years ago at our uncle Spurious George's bachelor party. Okay, I admit I drank too much, but what the heck. If you can't go crazy celebrating your uncle's wedding to a pretty, young white-headed capuchin, what's the world coming to, right?

What's the deal with Curious George anyway? Look at him with all that fame and fortune, not to mention all the lady monkeys waiting in line to kiss his hairy ass. We're not all that different from the outside, Curious George and me. And what did it get me? Nothing but a life of hardship and misery – or, as my ex-wife likes to say, a boatload of rotten bananas.

Curious George has everything. Me? Well, let's just say they don't call me Furious for nothing. I've tried yoga. And meditation. And pills prescribed to calm me down. Sometimes I mellow out for a minute or two, but one look at the news – one look at the messed-up world we live in – and I go bonkers! Cuckoo! Bat-guano crazy! You get the picture. It makes me so … so … so … furious!

About a year ago, I was locked up for disturbing the peace. I don't blame them. Hell, I'd lock me up. At least it's quiet here. But talk about crazy, I heard a rumor the other day that they're thinking about releasing me. I flew into a Kong-sized rage when I caught wind of that crap.

"We'll re-evaluate him in a few months," they said after tranquilizing me.

Sure, that's what they said, but I could see from the way they said it, and the way they glanced sideways at one another, I wasn't getting out anytime soon. That's just fine by me. Like I said, it's quiet here. And three meals a day isn't such a bad deal. By the way, don't let them tell you the food is bad. I mean, come on, it takes a lot to screw up bananas, right?

Getting back to Curious George, the thing that bugs me most is that he doesn't even appreciate his good fortune. I read an article the other day in the *Monkey Enquirer* about how he wasn't excited at all about his latest blockbuster movie deal. What an ingrate! And if I see one more story about how he's bored to death by the harem of cute little monkeys hanging on his every word, well that might put me over the edge for good. Then I'd have to once again remind everyone why it is they call me Furious.

Drunken Boat

The bar at the end of the pier was a rickety shack made of wood planks shining under the light of a nearly full moon. A malfunctioning red neon sign with the bar's name flickered and hissed in the late-night fog. With the "D" missing, it read "runken Boat."

I took a last drag off my cigarette, stomped it out on the pier, and pushed through the door. It took a second for my eyes to adjust. The only light in the room came from an old jukebox, a few fake candles, and a string of cheap red lights hanging from two wooden beams running the length of the room.

A large man called out from behind the bar. "We're closed."

I looked at the bartender and then at the five sketchy characters leaning on the bar-top.

"You don't look closed," I replied.

"See the sign," said the bartender, pointing to a placard saying they had the right to refuse service to anyone. "We don't serve pigs," he added for good measure.

"I'll take a hike soon enough," I said, "but first I need to ask a question."

"Make it quick, oinker."

"I'm trying to find Meatball," I called out. "Anyone seen him?"

No one looked up from the bar. No one so much as flinched. I might as well have been talking to the herd of seals down at the wharf. I reached into my coat pocket and pulled out a photograph of a man who was as short as he was wide, a two-bit, second-tier gangland character who went by the name of Meatball, though Cannonball would also have worked.

"I have a message for Meatball," I said, walking down the length of the bar.

"No one here knows about any Meatball," said the bartender. He reached down for a baseball bat and started to move out from behind the counter.

I could turn around and walk out the door, past the "runken Boat" sign, and be on my merry way. Or I could make a grab for the empty Anchor Steam bottle on the counter and put a permanent dent in the bartender's skull. This course of action, it occurred to me, would have put me on the losing end of a five-on-one ass-whooping.

Before I could make my next move, a door creaked open in the back of the bar, and a stocky man wearing a tuxedo walked into the room. He was followed by two gun-toting goons holding guns.

"I hear you're looking for Meatball," said the sharp-dressed man.

"That's right," I said.

"Well, you found him."

The Angel Who Bruised My Heart

There's a bruise on my heart that can't be healed. You may think I'm being overly dramatic, and I admit it kind of sounds like a line from one of those old Hank Williams songs like *Your Cheatin' Heart* or *I'm So Lonesome I Could Cry*. That might be the case, but it's also the truth. Or, as my one-legged grand-pappy used to say, "God's honest truth." I could spend hours shooting the shit about my one-legged grand-pappy, but that's not why we're here today, is it officer?

No, it isn't. So, I'll save that for another time. Maybe you'll read about it in the papers someday after the reporters wrangle my story into shape. Anyway, as for the unhealable bruise on my heart, that came from one woman and one woman alone. I'm not saying there weren't others. No, nothing like that. But when it comes to affairs of the heart, my friend, it all goes back to Constance (how's that for an ironic name?). Yeah, it was Constance, though you all know her now as Angel.

Angel. Do you want to know where that name came from? I'll tell you. It was the night I met her. The Fourth of July. In the year of our Lord nineteen hundred and seventy-three. I'd just gotten dropped off by a drive-all-night trucker who went by the name Jumpin' Jehoshaphat. He'd picked me up on an onramp outside of Salt Lake City and brought me all the way to Frisco.

Oh, you don't like that, do you? I can see it in your eyes. Alright, I get it. No more Frisco. Jumpin' Jehoshaphat transported me and two tons of frozen Angus beef all the way to San Francisco and let me off right in front of Bloom's Saloon. You know the place? Sure you do.

Anyway, I've never been one to pass up an old dive bar, especially back in those days. So I heaved my duffle bag onto my shoulder and sauntered on in. You know what? Right away I felt like I was right at home. The dim lights. The dart board. The pool table. The long wooden counter. The smell of spilt beer. And Jimi Hendrix wailing away on the jukebox. It was like I walked straight into dive bar heaven.

You got a cigarette? No, well, that's okay. I should quit anyway.

There wasn't but a handful of patrons in Blooms that night. I know now that the place can get busy on some nights. On that night, however, back in 1973, there was nothing going on. It was just me and some crusty barfly at the end of the counter, two old-timers shooting pool, and a lesbian couple staring out the back window at the Frisco skyline. Sorry, San Francisco.

As I hopped up on a stool, an inviting voice called out to me from behind the bar.

"What's your pleasure, stranger?"

I couldn't see much because of the way the lights played off the mirrors behind the bar and shined in my eyes – and remember this was after a number of days without very much sleep, with Jumpin' Jehoshaphat going on and on about the shady state of politics in our country. Whatever the reason, when I looked in the direction of the person speaking to me from behind the bar, it was like her whole body was surrounded by some kind of aura, some kind of mystical, or I might even say Biblical, light. From where I stood, it looked to me like she had a halo, not just on her head, but around her entire body.

"Well, Angel," I said, "ain't you a vision to behold."

That's exactly what I said the first time I saw her. And from that point on the name stuck. Angel. Now, some would ask me, and many have over the years, was she an angel of mercy or an angel of death? All I can say at this point, knowing what I know now, is that maybe she was a little bit of both.

But, hell, just listen to me yakking on like my one-legged grand-pappy. What exactly are we here to discuss, officer?

Ceasefire

Looking back at it now, the ceasefire was never going to work. Rigo and Camilla Ortiz had been married for six years, or as Rigo had grown accustomed to saying, "six very long years." But if you could step back in time and watch those years play out, you'd see the first five years had been amazing – the very picture of marital bliss. It was only in the last year or so that things got ugly.

"It was that stupid class," said Rigo to the marriage counselor. He was referring to the Introduction to Women's Literature course that Camilla attended at the local community college.

"It's just something to do for fun once a week," Camilla said at the time. "I like to learn new things."

To be fair to Rigo, he didn't have a problem with the fact that Camilla had signed up for school. Nor did he have a problem, at first, with her signing up for a course about women writers. The problem came when Camilla started holding Rigo's feet to the fire for every slight perpetrated by man – any and every man – against women.

"Holy crap," said Rigo to the counselor. "From the first night she came home from one of those classes, all she could talk about was how unfairly 'they'd' been treated by 'us.' 'Men have been our oppressor,' she said before hitting me with some major stink-eye, like it was all my fault."

It didn't take long for squabbles to escalate from skirmishes to battles, and then into all-out war. Rigo eventually came up with the idea of a "ceasefire" as a way of trying to save the marriage.

"Here's the deal," he said. "I love you, baby, but this isn't working. I don't want to fight with you."

"I'm not fighting," said Camilla. "I'm just sharing some information about my class."

"Yeah, but that's the problem."

Rigo knew he was treading on razor blades, but he'd made up his mind that this was the only path to a solution. He calmly laid out the terms of the ceasefire. As his part of the deal, he promised to be open-minded about Camilla's newfound feminist ideas. He also promised not to speak negatively about the literary ladies Camilla was learning about.

He figured it would be easy enough to keep up with his end of the bargain, especially if it meant harmony in the home. Things started well enough – with both sides keeping the peace – until about a week ago. On a cool autumn evening when Rigo thought Camilla was doing laundry in the garage, he was chatting on the phone to his brother.

"Dude," said Rigo, "those authors she goes on and on about sound like the biggest bunch of bitches. You know what I'm sayin'?"

Just as the words left his mouth, Rigo saw Camilla turn the corner. Faster than her husband could say "I'm in the doghouse now," she let him have it with both barrels.

"You can take that stupid ceasefire and shove it up your ass," she said.

"Come on, honey," he pleaded. "I thought you were in the garage. I …"

"I'm so out of here," she hissed. "Now you and your brother can sit around all day scratching your crotches and grunting like Neanderthals about all that stupid sports stuff that gets you off."

And with that, Camilla had violated her side of the treaty. For she had pledged, and had perfectly kept her word to this point, that she would not complain about Rigo's full-blown obsession with sports.

That's when the ceasefire ended for good. And it doesn't look like either side is all that interested in returning to the table to forge a lasting peace.

Speaking in Tongues

"I don't know what you're saying," I told the woman in the restaurant, "because you're speaking in tongues."

She kept talking as if I hadn't said a word, as if I wasn't even there.

"Excuse me," I said, trying a different tact. "Do you speak English? Français? Español?"

Did that register with her? Did anything register with her? It didn't seem to. She continued speaking in tongues.

I signaled for the skinny Ukrainian waiter by snapping my fingers in the air like a bigshot. Maybe she's speaking Ukrainian, I thought. Maybe he'll be able to tell me what she's saying.

I don't know if the waiter heard the snap of my fingers. I don't even know if he was paying any attention to me at all. He didn't seem to. Maybe it was because he was taking an order from another table, a large, circular table surrounded by a motley assortment of road-weary circus performers. Funny, I thought, I didn't know the circus was in town.

When he finished taking their order, the waiter rushed passed me like I wasn't even there. He's ignoring me, I thought. Or maybe he's avoiding the woman speaking in tongues. Or maybe he didn't like the way I snapped my fingers.

The waiter hurried through the swinging doors into the kitchen. Soon I heard voices – loud, angry, foreign voices. Are they talking about me? I wondered. Is the woman speaking in tongues talking about me?

Finally, the Ukrainian waiter came to my table.

"What took so long?" I asked him.

"I'm sorry, sir," he replied, with more than a hint of sarcasm. "May I take your order?"

"I don't even know what I want," I said. "I haven't had time to look at the menu, but can you please tell this woman to go away? Or, if she's speaking Ukrainian, tell me what she's saying."

The skinny waiter looked to the left, then to the right. He turned around completely to look behind his back. Then he faced me again.

"I don't know what you're talking about," he said. "There's no one else in the restaurant besides you and me."

Wish I Had Wings

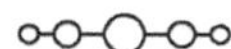

Connie Vict: I wish I had wings.

Jay L. Byrd: You're not the only one.

Connie: What's that supposed to mean?

Jay: (says nothing; looks at dirty fingernails)

Connie: I said … what's that supposed to mean?

Jay: It means that I wish you had wings, too. You'd fly away and we'd finally get some peace and quiet around here.

Connie: Man, if I had wings I'd be out of here so fast.

Jay:	You don't need wings to fly this chicken coop.
Connie:	Sure, I'll just bust through these bars and walk out. And hope that crazy sheriff doesn't shoot me on the way through the gate.
Jay:	Maybe he'll get lucky and put a bullet in your ass.
Connie:	You and your stupid jokes. Someday, man, I'd really like to take a swing at you.
Jay:	What's stopping you?
Connie:	Solitary … that's what's stopping me. Can't stand that stinking hole.
Jay:	(says nothing)
Connie:	Seriously, I'd rather be in here with you than alone in the hole.
Jay:	I hear you.
Connie:	Effing hole.
Jay:	Effing hole.
Connie:	If only we had wings.
Jay:	I'd fly to Chicago. See my girl.
Connie:	Shit, I'd make a beeline straight for the border. Tijuana here I come!

Jay: Yeeha.

Connie: Wait, you're saying you'd go to Chicago if you could fly anywhere in the world?

Jay: That's right.

Connie: That's stupid.

Jay: What do you mean? My family lives on the south side.

Connie: Oh, your family that never writes to you, your family that's never even written once, that family?

Jay: At least I have a family. And don't say anything about that hooker who writes to you from Tuscaloosa. She's only after your money.

Connie: (says nothing)

Jay: Only you don't have any money, bro. Wait 'til she finds that out. That'll be the last time she visits your sorry ass.

Connie: Man, don't talk like that about my lady.

Jay: Ha, she's gonna be the one wearing wings when she learns you're broke.

Connie: Shut up, man. I'm trying to sleep.

Jay: Good idea. Go to sleep.

Connie: I will when you stop talking.

Jay: Okay … I'm done talking. Good night,
               Con.

Connie: Good night, Jay.

Sorting through the Trash

I was sorting through the garbage before going to work. God, I thought, it's already been a long day and I haven't even had my first cup of coffee. I dug my hands further into the trashcan, rifling through the refuse while narrowly avoiding the jagged edge of the discarded metal can of Del Monte peach halves. "Where is it?" I whispered. "Where's that stupid scrap of paper?" Something rancid made me back away from the can and glance at the clock. "Shit." I muttered, "This can't be happening. Not today of all days."

I lifted the bin and dumped the contents on the kitchen floor. The sour-smelling heap of trash included many papers, soiled and otherwise. And empty food containers, also soiled and otherwise. On one side of the pile, four crushed leftover boxes from last week's visit to Szechuan Temple stuck out like the diorama of a rural Chinese village half-buried by a landslide. Dark rivulets of week-old soy sauce filled in the crags and pores of grout between the kitchen tiles. "Please Jesus," I moaned. "Please don't do this to me?" And then I shouted, "Where's the damned paper?"

My voice boomed in the hollow space of the empty apartment, not that anyone could hear me, except for maybe the Thai couple next door. But they wouldn't be up yet anyway and I doubt any noise I made could rouse them from their drug-addled nightmares. "Crackheads," I spat, then glared again at the clock. "At least they have each other."

Maybe that was the root of my entire problem. Maybe if I lived with someone I'd have an organized filing system. Maybe if I lived with someone, I'd pin notes to a corkboard designed to hold important messages. Maybe if I lived with someone, I'd finally get around to buying separate bins for trash (white), and recycling (blue), and compost (green). Maybe if I lived with someone, I wouldn't be on my knees right now rummaging through the foul-smelling landslide-ravaged remains of the Szechuan Temple. But that's exactly where I was, pawing through the trash like some two-bit lowlife before starting the first day of my new job.

"I'm pretty sure it was Third Street," I said while scrounging for the scrap of paper on which I'd scribbled the name, address, and phone number of my new workplace. I'd never set foot in the building and had only spoken on the phone once to the mailroom supervisor.

I clawed once more through the pile before giving up.

"Forget it," I said, leaving the trash heap behind as I shuffled slowly, but with a clear sense of purpose, toward the crack pipe stashed behind the cleaning supplies in my bathroom cabinet.

In the Shadows

We only meet in the shadows. It's safer this way.

That's not to say there isn't risk. I know people who've been picked up coming from or going to the shadows. Sometimes they return roughed up, with a black eye here, a broken arm there. More often, though, they don't come back at all.

I heard a story recently about a student leader at the local university. He was rounded up on his way to a meeting in the shadows and hasn't been heard from since. His mother still roams the streets asking if anyone has seen her son.

The other day, she pulled me aside to ask if she should go to the police.

"I wouldn't do that," I said. "It's too dangerous."

I saw a glassy, faraway look in her eyes, as though she knew time was running out for her boy.

I was once brought in for questioning, though I never knew why. They released me after a few hours, but only after beating me enough to let me know I was on their radar.

When my wife asked where I'd been, I told her I had to work late. That didn't explain the bruises, but she knew not to probe any further. I didn't want her to worry. I also didn't want her to know about the meetings in the shadows.

It's safer this way.

Sacrifice

The kicking and the screaming are over now. She'd tried everything to escape – pleading, punching, scratching, even biting. In the end, she's just one woman, and they have numbers on their side.

She's limp, drained of energy and sapped of spirit. She remembers the red, hot liquid they forced down her throat. Scalding and sticky, the potion smelled and tasted of blood, but it eventually calmed her, numbed her, resigned her to her plight and, in a way, set her free. The heavy ropes around her arms and legs no longer burned her flesh, no longer made her want to cry out.

Two sentries watch her from the passageway, the only way into or out of the temple chamber. In a matter of hours, at daybreak, her fate awaits her. Villagers from miles around will come, dressed in ceremonial robes and adorned with the ritual jewelry they wear for these occasions. The acolytes will undress me, she thinks, and lead me to the altar at the top of the temple steps. If I can't walk on my own, they'll hoist me onto their shoulders and carry me.

The ceremonial chants from the villagers gathered around the temple base will rise with the wind. And in the warmth of the new day's sun, those in attendance will quiver with excitement over the spectacle they're about to witness. I've been in their place, she thinks. Men and women alike will chant, though the women will be louder, knowing they've been spared for another year.

When the high priest arrives, he'll climb to the stone altar on bloodied hands and knees. Those below will temporarily shift their gaze away from me, thinks the woman, to watch the holy man's slow ascent. Then they'll focus on me again when he reaches the top. This is the sacred union they've been praying for, the holy matrimony when the high priest reaches heavenwards and plunges the sacrificial blade into my heavily sedated heart.

The Endeavour

Night was coming fast. And the *Endeavour* was long overdue.

It wouldn't have been strange for the ship to be a few minutes late, but not two hours. I squinted up at the arctic slush shimmering under the rays of the midnight sun. It won't get much darker than this, I thought. But it will get a lot colder. I fought the urge to shiver, as if I could gird myself against the dropping temperature. Who was I fooling?

This had all started as a routine assignment. As one of the ship's senior guides, I'd been put ashore to scout the location for tomorrow's hike on this barren glacier. The captain, in the meantime, would treat our passengers to a short cruise along a nearby sea cliff housing millions of screeching, squawking migratory seabirds. Yes, it had all been very routine – until the radio went out.

The batteries must have died, I figured. It's a good thing we had already agreed to a rendezvous time.

I adjusted the strap of my binoculars hanging around my neck. What else did I have? An old hunting rifle. Four bullets. A compass given to me by my wife as an anniversary gift. A handful of stale Norwegian biscuits. And a malfunctioning radio. I surveyed the vast, desolate expanse of ice and water all around me.

I removed my gloves and tapped the radio with my fingertips. Nothing. Scanning the empty strait, I noticed a solitary black seal lift its head out of the choppy water, stare at me with its large, black eyes, and slowly sink beneath the surface.

A burst of static came from the radio. Then a voice. Barely audible.

"Mayday. Mayday. Endeavour in trouble. Lifeboats deployed. Mayday. May ..."

The radio went out again. I pressed the "TALK" button on and off, on and off. Nothing. I shook the radio and banged it hard against my palm.

Nothing.

Breakfast with the Alien

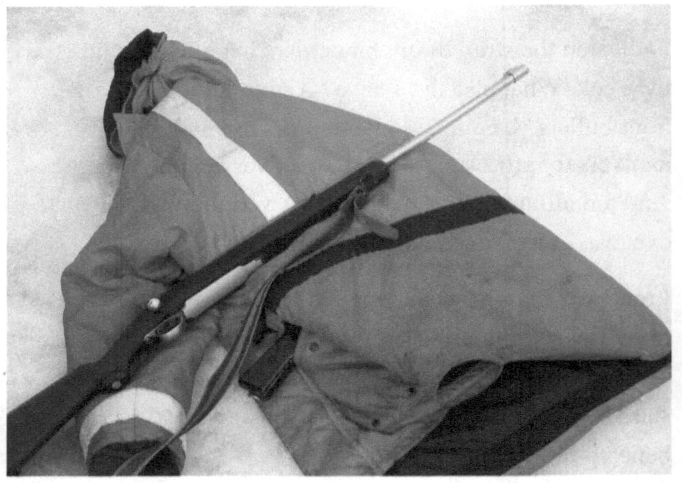

One Bag or Two

The boy from *The Shining* was bagging the groceries. No doubt about it. He was older now. But he had the same bowl haircut, the same small brown eyes and rounded pudgy face, though it was puffy and tired-looking now.

"Paper or plastic?" the boy asked each customer as they reached the front of the line. "One bag or two?"

I contemplated changing lines, but they were all much longer and I was running late, so I stuck it out. Maybe he'll move to another line, I hoped. As I stood there waiting to be checked out, I thought back to the first time I saw that movie on the big screen at the Coronet theater in San Francisco.

For months afterwards, I walked around saying "redrum, redrum" and speaking to my bent index finger like it was my imaginary best friend. My mother wasn't amused. She kept telling me to stop and eventually brought me to a shrink who asked a lot of probing questions that I answered with monosyllabic responses and shoulder shrugs. The thing I remember most about him was his annoying habit of scratching the backs of his hands throughout our conversation. After a few visits with Dr. Itchyhands, I stopped saying "redrum."

"Paper," I said to *The Shining* man before he could ask me. "Two bags."

Instead of getting the bags ready, he just stared at me with those sad, small, beady, brown eyes.

"Two bags," I repeated.

He smiled, held up his bent finger, and whispered "redrum."

"Redrum?" I asked.

"Redrum," he said again.

We went back and forth with "redrum" after "redrum" after "redrum," each time getting a little louder like two bickering crows.

It didn't take long for everyone else to back away and look at us like we were a couple of lunatics.

When the police came, I was surprised they didn't arrest *The Shining* man as well. It takes two to tango, I wanted to tell the officers as they led me out of the store. But when I looked back toward the checkout line, I saw that *The*

Shining man was gone. An old woman had taken his place as the bagger.

Later, during the trial, I listened as the prosecutor told the court about how they found my mother's body. My lawyer instructed me not to say a word, so I didn't. But if I could I would have spoken the only word running around my head and the only thing I say now while sitting on my bunk in solitary – "redrum."

Reporting Back

… as you've heard in previous transmissions, the first few months of the mission went as planned. After setting up our basecamp, we explored the area and conducted experiments to prove the theory that Septima Dark was indeed an ideal colonization opportunity.

As communications officer, it was my duty to report the details of our mission back to Earth. You'll know by now that things began to unravel after our first forays across the ashen terrain of the dark zone. We lost contact with Commander Middleton's team during a five-day reconnaissance mission. Eventually, only Dr. Stevens returned, but she was barely alive when she stumbled into camp.

We brought Stevens to the infirmary, but she never recovered enough to tell us what happened in the dark zone. When she died a few days later, we performed a detailed autopsy – it showed nothing – and incinerated her remains. What we didn't know was that the disease she carried into camp had already spread.

We tried to find a cure, but the virus moved too quickly. One by one, the crew transformed into unrecognizable creatures that fed on each other's flesh. I alone was immune. I never figured out why.

In the chaos of the days that followed the outbreak, I hid in the communications cell while the creatures turned and fell upon each other. There came a time, however, when they stopped attacking each other and instead focused on hunting me down. It was like a contest to see who could get me first.

Late last night, when all was quiet in the camp, I ventured out to find food. As soon as I entered the commissary, I realized it was a trap. I barely made it back to my cell, but now they've seen where I'm holed up. Two creatures are stationed outside the portal, their stench coming through the crack under the door. An hour or so ago, the warning indicator lit up to let me know the oxygen generator is malfunctioning. I don't have much time.

Here are a few final words before they break through. Whatever you do, don't send another mission to Septimus Dark. As perfect as it looks from afar, there's something here that cannot be controlled. It would be better to blow this planet to kingdom come. Even if you …

At that point, the transmission cut off.

"What do you make of it?" asked Commander Levins.

"Well, at least we know they were sending reports," said the second-in-command, a veteran space explorer named Sanders, "though we still don't know why we never received them."

"I mean what do you make of his story?" said Levins.

"We've swept the camp," said Sanders. "There's no evidence of any creatures or any virus."

"Or any crew," said the commander.

"Affirmative," confirmed Sanders. "We haven't found any sign of the crew."

"Is the camp secure?" asked Levins.

"Yes, sir."

"Okay, post a guard on every building. It's been a long journey," said the commander. "We'll get a fresh start in the morning."

As Sanders barked orders into his communicator, he looked across the basecamp toward the shadowy entrance of the dark zone. For an instant, he thought he saw something move in the pitch-black space beyond the arc lights of the camp. Sanders rubbed his eyes, squinted to focus, and peered again into the darkness. There wasn't anything out there. The commander's right, he thought, it's been a long day and I need some shuteye. Before returning to the control center, Sanders lifted his binoculars for a last scan of the area. That's when he noticed the movement again, only this time he knew he wasn't imagining things. It was hard to make out any details, but Sanders clearly saw the slowly moving shape of someone – or something – emerging from the darkness.

"Halt," shouted Sanders.

Whoever or whatever it was shuffled forward, ignoring his command. By now, Sanders was also spooked by what sounded like a low rumbling growl coming from the intruder.

"Halt," Sanders ordered again. "Stand down or I'll shoot."

Sanders lifted his rifle and got the target in his sights. That's when he realized there was something familiar about the creature. He's undergone such a transformation, thought Sanders, as he prepared to squeeze the trigger, but this monstrous thing was once a man. And not just any man, Sanders understood, but the communications officer from the previous mission or what was left of him.

Two Birds, One Stone

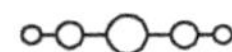

The forecast called for rain, but so far the skies were clear.

From his vantage point on the roof, Chet Larkins could see straight into the seventh-floor corner apartment of the building across the street. His job was easy enough. A doe-eyed blonde heiress with money to burn showed up at his office a few weeks ago wanting to know if her fiancé was getting a little something on the side. For a grand a day plus expenses, Larkins was hired to see if there was any dirt to dig up on hubby-to-be before Miss Doe-Eyes made a major matrimonial misstep.

"It'll be my third marriage," she said to Larkins. "I'm not in the mood for a third divorce."

Cases like these are usually straightforward, thought Larkins as he looked through his high-powered binoculars.

The guy is either fooling around or he isn't – it's usually as black and white as that. But there are exceptions; those times when you're thrown a real knee-buckler of a curve. Larkins realized early on this was going to be one of those cases.

The first thing he did when Doe-Eyes left his office was put a tail on her. It was standard operating procedure in Larkins's book. He needed to make sure she was who she said she was, make sure there were no surprises. It didn't take long to find out the honey-faced heiress wasn't as innocent as she appeared. While Doe-Eyes was busy hiring a private investigator to follow her fiancé, she was rolling around in the mud herself. Larkins filed away that little tidbit for later if needed.

As for Mr. About-to-Be-Married, he wasn't just having any old affair. Not only was the dirty dog cozying up to the Mayor's wife, but he was also sneaking around with the eldest daughter of the city's biggest crime boss. Who's it going to be tonight, Mrs. Mayor or Little Miss Mobster? Larkins wondered. He lowered the glasses to give his eyes a rest and noticed the clouds blowing in from the west. Looks like we might get some rain after all, he thought.

Little did Chet Larkins, private investigator, know that he wouldn't have to worry about putting on his raincoat. On a neighboring rooftop, tucked away beneath a neon "Jesus Saves" sign, a hitman named Louis Carvell had Larkins in his sights. Easy money, thought Carvell, as he squeezed the trigger to earn the first half of his payment. The hired gun would earn the second half later that night when he took care of the fiancé.

Unfortunately for Larkins, Doe-Eyes had found out about his extracurricular snooping. She was a private person and wanted to keep it that way. In her mind, there was only one way to fix the problems she was having with the private eye and her dearly beloved rat-fink of a fiancé.

As she put it when handing over the cash to Carvell, "This is what you call killing two birds with one stone."

Hey Mister

"Hey mister," I called out from my lookout spot near the garbage cans. It smelled like rotten bananas, but it was the only place where I could stay out of the clerk's line of sight. "Hey mister," I called out again, but the man kept walking.

"Asshole," I muttered under my breath.

I looked over at the Country Squire parked across the street and shrugged my shoulders as if to say "this is a waste of time," but Sal and Jesse raised their hands to signal for me to wait for the next person. Alright, I thought, I'll stick it out, but this is a terrible way to spend the night. Serves me right, I also thought, for growing this poor excuse for a mustache.

"It makes you look older than us," Jesse had said.

I ducked back behind the garbage cans and waited, and it wasn't long before a guy pulled up in a dark-blue Camaro Z28.

"Hey mister," I said when he got out of the car.

He stopped and looked around, then kept walking toward the store.

"Over here," I said a little louder.

He turned and came toward me slowly, his black boots kicking up gravel that pinged off the metal trashcans.

"What's going on, kid?" he asked.

"Can you buy me a six pack?"

"Get out of here," he laughed. "Are you nuts?"

"No," I said. "I left my ID at home, so I'm looking for a little help." As I talked, I stuck my upper lip forward, making sure he saw my scraggly mustache.

"Nice try," he said, "but I'm not falling for that crap."

He turned toward the front door of the store.

"I'll make it worth your while," I said. It sounded more like a question than a statement. The man stopped and looked over his shoulder.

"What do you have in mind?"

"I'll give you twenty bucks," I offered.

"Plus a six pack for me?" he said, more as a statement than a question.

"What? That's BS!"

"Okay then," he turned again. "I'll be seeing you."

"Wait," I called out too loudly. "It's a deal. Twenty bucks plus a six pack."

I pulled two crumpled twenties from my shirt pocket.

"This is how it's going to work," said the man, pocketing my money without looking at it. "Meet me in ten minutes around the corner by the post office. I'll bring the beer and your change."

"What?" I nearly shouted. "How can I trust you?"

"You can't," said the man, "but you don't have much choice, do you?"

When I returned to the Country Squire, Sal and Jesse were pissed off at first when I told them how the deal went down, but they soon agreed there wasn't much else I could do.

"We always run a certain amount of risk in these transactions," said Sal, who had a tendency for being philosophical.

"It's all good," Jesse agreed.

An hour or so later, long after we all realized the Dark-Blue Camaro guy had taken us for a ride, we were parked in front of the post office talking about what to do next.

"This sucks," I said, "I'm going home."

"Wait a minute," said Jesse, pulling a pair of twenties out of his wallet. "The night's still young."

"Yeah, let's give it one more shot," Sal chimed in and handed over a twenty of his own.

Part of me wanted to get as far away as I could from my numbskull friends, but I was also attracted to the idea of trying one more time, especially since I'd be using their money this time around.

When a lime-green Karmann Ghia pulled into the store parking lot, I stroked my mustache with my thumb and index finger and took a deep breath.

"Hey mister," I called before realizing the driver was a dark-haired woman wearing a short, tight-fitting skirt.

"Well, well," she said, her high heels crunching on the gravel as she moved toward me. "What do we have here?"

With the cold beer in my lap, I buckled up and sat back as the woman put the Karmann Ghia in gear. "So long, suckers," I wanted to shout at Sal and Jesse when we roared past the Country Squire, but I kept my mouth shut and thought instead about how this night wasn't going to be such a waste of time after all.

In Chinatown

Late last week, my grandfather said, "In Chinatown, the turtles are alive."

"That's interesting," I replied to humor him, "I didn't know there were turtles in Chinatown."

"Well there are," he said loudly, "and they're alive."

Sometimes there wasn't any explanation for what grandpa said or did. Was he losing his marbles, or was it too many sleeping pills? Or maybe it was a combination of both. As my ex-girlfriend liked to say, "A + B = Wacko."

But sometimes he could be crystal clear. When he told me "the turtles are alive," he seemed lucid as a right-minded Supreme Court Justice. And, just to be clear, by "right-minded," I mean someone who thinks in the correct manner, as opposed to someone who leans to the right.

A few nights later, on Halloween, while we sat in the near-dark living room listening to *The Sorcerer's Apprentice*, he insisted on playing the record on the turntable even though I had the music on CD.

"You can't beat the audio quality of vinyl," he said.

"Yeah," I replied, "but records are so fragile."

"Technology is the devil," he countered, his tone of voice indicating that he was through with this conversation.

As soon as I lowered the stylus onto the vinyl, he was up and dancing around the dimly lit room, swinging his arms to the music and stomping around like he was the sorcerer's apprentice performing chores for his master.

I got a kick out of his sudden burst of energy, though I could imagine that Mrs. Windsock in the apartment below wasn't too amused.

"Don't break a hip," I said, only half-joking.

"I love this music," shouted my grandfather. "And I love that it's on vinyl."

As he pranced from one side of the living room to the other, I had a vision of him as a young man, sweeping my grandmother or any number of other enchanted women off their feet at some dime-a-dance ballroom.

The music built as layer upon layer of instruments worked their way toward the orchestral climax. Then, without warning, the needle stuck in a groove and the record skipped. Seemingly in time to the music, or more accurately, in time to the skip in the music, my grandfather grabbed at his chest and fell to the floor with a loud thump.

If old Mrs. Windsock wasn't annoyed before, she certainly would be now after my grandfather's collapse made the entire room shake.

I scrambled off the couch to switch on the overhead light, though what I saw made me wish I'd left it off. My grandfather, still grabbing at his chest with one hand, writhed on the floor in convulsions so violent I thought at first they couldn't be real. He's pulling a Halloween gag on me, I imagined. But it didn't take long to realize this wasn't a joke.

While waiting for the ambulance, I knelt by my grandfather's side and caught a heavy whiff of Wild Turkey. How did he sneak that stuff into the house? I wondered. He wasn't supposed to be drinking any booze.

I felt for his hand. "Grandpa," I said. "Can you hear me?"

There was no response.

"Grandpa," I called a little louder.

He squeezed my hand then, and with a big smile on his face, said, "In Chinatown, the turtles are alive."

The Thrashing

And when the rebellion was over, the rebel leader emerged from the jungle with torn clothes and bloody knuckles. Smiling broadly, he thanked those who fought hard for his victory – "our victory," he called it – though everyone knew what he meant. It was his victory most of all.

"To the victor, the spoils," he shouted to his comrades.

He spoke, too, to the vanquished, about the need to mend fences. "You've been a worthy foe," he said, urging his supporters to swallow their unveiled insults. "To you who were once against us," he continued, placing his hands on his chest. "To you, I offer an olive branch. We must forge ahead together to form a more perfect union."

The weary enemies before him were bruised and battered, but they were also heartened by what they heard. "Maybe this can work," they muttered among themselves as they laid down their arms and found it in their wounded hearts to accept, in good faith, his words of peace and healing.

Little did they know, however, that before delivering his victory speech, the rebel leader had held a meeting with his top commanders and closest advisors to dictate his first executive order, a decree to immediately build the largest death camp in the world.

"This will be our final victory," he'd said to his followers before making a slashing motion across his throat to ensure they all understood the full intent of his words.

The Milling Crowd

The tension rose in the milling crowd as the election results poured in. It started as a dull murmur, a low-level hum that surged like a rolling wave.

"What just happened?" people asked. "Who did we elect? Did anyone really vote for this guy?"

When news reports confirmed the unfathomable, everyone in the crowd shook their heads as if to say "it wasn't me."

The murmur got louder when a small group at the back of the crowd rose their arms to take credit.

"Woohoo," they cheered. "We voted for him."

Boos and curses were hurled down on this group like rocks. Someone, deciding insults weren't enough, picked up a metal object and threw it indiscriminately into the crowd. The object struck the 75-year-old mother of a man openly carrying an AK-47 assault rifle, which were now legal throughout the land.

Ignoring his bleeding mother, the man raised his rifle and fired off a burst in the direction of the assailant, not that he knew who had thrown the metal object.

All hell broke loose as soon as the gunshots started. People in the crowd lifted their weapons and began firing, some in retaliation and some in support of the injured old lady and her son. People clawed and gouged and kicked to escape the massacre – or at least try to. The dull murmur transformed into a bloodcurdling roar.

All the while, the newly elected leader, brushing his hair from his eyes, grabbed a handful of cheese-flavored popcorn and marveled at the spectacle.

"Isn't it great," he said to those sitting with him in the bulletproof suite. "This is exactly what our country needs."

Welcome Home

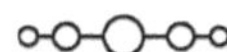

Jim walks into his apartment and it's completely different – furniture, décor all changed. No one's home.

Jim: Hello…

No response. He looks around the living room.

Jim: Hello (louder). Mama? You here, Mama?

The walls of the room are painted yellow. They used to be blue.

Jim: Mama, are you here? (looks at the walls) What a godawful color.

Still no response. Jim pauses, wondering for a second if he's in the wrong apartment, but then looks down at his keys.

Jim: No, this is our place. My keys still work.

He looks around some more and sees his favorite recliner on the wrong side of the room.

Jim: What the hell's going on here?

He hears a key in the lock and looks toward the door.

Jim: Mama, is that you?

A large man opens the door and stares at Jim. Jim stares back.

Large man: Who are you?

Jim: That's what I was going to ask you.

The large man goes to a large dresser, opens a drawer, and pulls out a pistol.

Large man: I'm not going to ask again. Who are you?
                 And what are you doing in my place?

Jim: Your place? What are you talking about?
                 This is my apartment. What'd you do with
                 my mama?

Large man: Mama? Who's mama? I bought the
                 place fully furnished four years ago
                 from a toothless geezer named Rufus
                 Underbright.

The large man gestures with the pistol.

Large man: Who are you anyway?

Jim: My name's Jim. I lived here with my mama. I just got out of the joint today and wanted to surprise her.

The large man lowers the gun a little bit.

Large man: I'm telling you there's no mama here.

Jim: Where is she? (Jim asks himself.)

The large man lowers the gun all the way.

Large man: Hey, you want some tea?

Jim: No response.

Large man: Jasmine or Earl Grey?

Jim: What?

Large man: I said do you want a cup of tea? It might calm you down a little.

Jim: Okay. Earl Grey.

The large man goes into the kitchen. We hear the sound tea being prepared (cabinets opening and closing, water running, kettle boiling).

Jim: (to himself) I can't believe he painted the walls yellow.

He sits in his chair on the wrong side of the room.

Large man: (from the kitchen) You say something?

Jim: Nothing.

Jim gets up, looks toward the kitchen, picks up his chair, and puts it in the "right place." The large man returns with the tea and does a double-take when he sees the chair on the other side of the room.

Jim: This is where my chair goes.

Large man: Here's your tea.

He hands the cup to Jim.

Jim: Thanks man. You know what?

Large man: What?

Jim: (He looks around the walls.) I like what you've done to the place.

Large man: Thanks.

Jim: Yeah, even the color is starting to grow on me.

Monster Mash

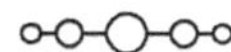

"I want to suck your blood," said the Count in his most menacing-yet-seductive voice.

"Back off, Drac," warned the Wolfman. "Not even a bloodsucker of your caliber wants to have anything to do with my tainted hemoglobin."

"Yeah, but look on the bright side," said Dracula. "At least you have a killer howl."

"Aaarrgghhh," groaned the Frankenstein monster in what might have been a laugh.

"Mmmmmnnnn," added the Mummy.

"Listen to those guys," replied the Wolfman. "I didn't know you were such a comedian, Dracula. You're gonna have these two goons rolling on the floor before long."

"Are you sure they're laughing?"

"Could be," said the Wolfman. "Maybe we need to hire a translator."

"Maybe you should post an ad on Craigslist," said a disembodied voice.

The four monsters looked at each other to figure out who spoke those words.

"Wasn't me," said Dracula, picking something out of his top right fang.

"Me either," said the Wolfman.

Frankenstein and the Mummy both shook their heads and shrugged their shoulders as if to say, "Don't look at us."

"Wait a minute," said Dracula. He squinted as if that gave him a magical power to see the unseen.

"Are you thinking what I'm thinking?" asked the Wolfman.

"Yes, indeed," said Dracula, who then spoke aloud to no one in particular. "Invisible Man, is that you?"

A hearty laugh erupted in the room.

"Nice work, Sherlock," said the voice. "I was wondering when one of you numbskulls would figure it out."

"I really wish you wouldn't sneak around like that," said the Wolfman. "It creeps me out."

"Try looking at yourself in the mirror during a full moon sometime," the Invisible Man shot back. "Now that's something to be creeped out about."

Frankenstein and the Mummy snickered.

"I have to agree with Wolfie on this one," the Count chimed in. "It's not nice to sneak up on us like you do."

"Are you kidding me?" blurted the Invisible Man. "If either one of you indiscriminate man-eaters knew where I was, you'd jump at the first chance to dine on my flesh and drink my blood. Just because I'm invisible doesn't mean I don't taste good."

"You're quite right, Invisible Man," agreed Dracula. "Invisible blood is as good as any other blood as far as I'm concerned."

"Er … do you guys want to go to the party?" asked the Wolfman, looking to change the subject and cut the tension.

"Why not," said Dracula, "but I sure hope it's not an all-vegetarian buffet like last year."

Frankenstein and the Mummy began growling at the prospect of a meatless night.

"Don't worry, boys," reassured the Wolfman. "We'll leave that boring party early to look for something more appetizing to dine on, if you know what I'm saying."

"All right, then," said Dracula. "What are we waiting for? Let's get out of here!"

"After you," said the Invisible Man, holding the door open for the four other monsters before turning out the light and following them to the Halloween party at the haunted castle across the street.

Smoked Pig

The charred smell of smoked pig hung in the damp jungle air. Everyone sang, except Leilana, who hung back from the fire pit, shielding her eyes from the thick smoke.

"Are you ready for some pig?" asked grandfather, patting the young girl's head.

The seven-year-old shot him a glance that made her displeasure known.

"What's that look, little one? Does the smoke hurt your eyes?"

"No," said Leilana, gritting her teeth and pursing her lips.

"Suit yourself," said grandfather before rejoining the circle of singers.

As the clan clustered around the smoky pit, Leilana edged toward the jungle. With each small step, the smoke cleared and the pig song became fainter and fainter.

"Little one!" she heard grandfather call. "Don't wander too far away."

"I won't," she answered, though she'd already stepped onto the path between the big-leaved trees and could hear the waves breaking on the shore. That's where I'll go, she thought.

When Leilana reached the beach, she was greeted by flames flickering in the night like hundreds of cat's eyes. She looked up and down the coast, amazed by the number of fires, each one representing a pig roasting in the ground. Turning her gaze to the ocean, Leilana stared out at the lights of a freighter drifting across the water like a ghost ship. She knew from grandfather that it was bound for somewhere like Europe or China or the United States.

That's where I'll go someday, thought Leilana as she tracked the ship's path across the dark line of the horizon.

"Where are you, little one?" grandfather shouted.

"Leilana … Leilana," others were also calling out to her.

Before she could respond, Leilana saw the leaves part and grandfather emerge from the thick jungle. He rushed forward and scooped her up in his bare arms.

"I told you to stay close." He hugged her tight. "We were all worried."

Seeing that all was well, the singers gathered around and began to chant the pig song. Soon their voices were so loud that Leilana could no longer hear the waves. Grandfather felt her shaking in his arms.

"What's the matter, girl?" he asked. "You're safe now."

"I want to get down," she cried. "I can walk on my own."

Grandfather put her on the ground and shook his head. "Sometimes I just don't know what gets into you, little one."

Leilana wiped the tears from her eyes and looked back one last time at the freighter in the distance.

Grandfather shrugged and the singers became quiet.

"That's where I'll go someday," said the young girl, pointing toward the ship, "and I'm not eating that pig."

She turned to walk on her own back to the fire pit.

Catharsis

The sign over the door read "catharsis" in lettering so faded it was barely legible. I must have come to the wrong place, I thought at first. There wasn't any light or sound or anything coming from inside. I pointed my flashlight app on the piece of paper in my hand to illuminate the note I'd received two hours earlier. There wasn't any mention of "catharsis." It was just an address and brief instructions.

"Bring ten thousand dollars in unmarked bills. Come alone and tell them Johnny sent you." That was it. That and this address.

A late model black Oldsmobile with tinted windows cruised up slowly and stopped across the street. A voice in my head asked, "what have you gotten yourself into now?"

I pushed the doorbell. If it made any sound, I didn't hear it.

No ring, no buzz, no chime. Nothing. I checked my watch. It was quarter past one in the morning. I'm getting too old for this, I thought and yawned. I'll wait five minutes, then I'm calling the cops. Just then the door creaked open and a short, bald man with a massive forehead and a thick, dark goatee came out to greet me. He was wearing a yellow jumpsuit with black stripes like Bruce Lee's outfit in *Game of Death*.

"Looking for something?" asked the short man.

"Johnny sent me," I said, giving him the line from the note.

"Which Johnny?" he said, "I know a lot of Johnnys."

In all my years as a private investigator there were only a few times I was sorry I didn't carry a gun. This was one of them. I calculated the striking distance between myself and the short man and gauged my chances of taking him out. Shouldn't be too difficult, I thought. At the same time, I kept going back to something my old jujitsu instructor used to say. "Explosive surprises often come in small packages," he'd say. I shifted my weight forward on the balls of my feet.

"Don't be an idiot," warned the short man. The sound of his knuckles cracking led me to notice the size of his sledgehammer fists. He pulled up his sleeves to show off his muscular forearms.

Who is this guy, I thought, Popeye's evil dwarf brother?

"Johnny sent me," I said again, this time more forcefully.

The short man stared at me for a minute. I wondered if he was plotting an assault on my kneecaps or an uppercut to my balls. Then, out of nowhere, a wide grin broke across his face and he let out a massive belly laugh.

"You're looking for Johnny?" he said. "Why didn't you say so?"

Before I could say, "I did say so, you moron," he motioned dramatically with his bulging arms and huge hands for me to come inside.

I hesitated for a second before passing under the faded sign.

"'Catharsis?'" I asked the short man. "What is this place?"

"Don't worry about it," he said while shutting and bolting the door. "You'll find out soon enough."

Down by the River

"Down by the river, I shot my baby."

Lester turned up the volume on his iPhone while walking down the dirt path toward the river bank. He held a folding chair in one hand and a small styrofoam cooler in the other.

As Neil Young launched into a blistering guitar solo, Lester bobbed his head back and forth to the hard-rocking rhythm. Down by the river, he thought, that's where I'm going.

He cranked up the volume as loud as it could go, but it still didn't take his mind off the one thing he'd been trying to forget. He and Alma had been married for 16 years. "Sixteen wonderful years," he liked to tell people when describing his marriage. In fact, everything had been wonderful until she landed the job at the bank.

"Down by the river ..."

From the first day, it was one late night after another. And just when Lester got used to his wife's crazy hours, she started working on the weekends, too. As much as Lester tried to convince himself that Alma's new job was a good thing for the family, it was clear she'd gone somewhere far, far away.

And then one day, by accident, he figured it out.

"Down by the river …"

He hadn't intended on spying on his wife. Not really. It just happened that way. One evening, on the way home from work, Lester stopped by the bank to see if Alma wanted to join him for dinner. In the old days, she would have been thrilled by a surprise visit. When he pulled into the parking lot, however, he arrived just in time to see his wife get into a car with Humbert, the bank manager.

"Down by the river …"

Following closely behind, but not too closely, Lester watched as they drove straight for the Best Western out by the airport.

That's all he needed to know.

"Down by the river …"

When he got home, Lester began plotting. He'd go down to the river with nothing but his favorite beach chair, a cooler packed with ice-cold Bud, and his favorite Smith & Wesson.

Down by the river, Lester wasn't going to shoot his baby. Down by the river, Lester was going to shoot himself.

Black Bird

The large crow shouted from the wire. "Your time has come," it yelled. "Your time has come."

I kept walking, hoping that by ignoring the black bird it would stop harassing me.

"Your time has come," it shouted louder than before. "Your time has come."

When I turned the corner, the persistent crow flew after me and landed on another section of the wire.

"Your time has come."

I stopped in my tracks, picked up a golf-ball-sized rock, and made a motion as if to hurl it at the bird.

"Ha ha," it said. "You'll never hit me."

I cocked my arm and threw the rock as hard as I could.

The crow laughed when the rock sailed wide right. "Your time has come," it said again.

"Shut up," I shouted and continued walking down the street.

I picked up my pace, knowing that if I made it home I could lock myself inside and be rid of my fine-feathered enemy once and for all. Only two more blocks, I thought. I can make it.

The crow continued flying after me, landing on one length of the wire after another and harassing me the entire way.

Damn bird, I thought, if only I had a gun.

"Your time has come," it shouted again as I turned onto the street where I live. Instead of following me, the bird took off from the wire and flew in the opposite direction. After all that, I thought, the stupid bird decides to fly away just when I'm about to reach the peace and quiet of home.

My key was already in my hand by the time I walked up the steps to my front door. As I turned the door handle, I heard a loud whooshing sound coming from behind, and I turned just in time to see the large black bird coming straight for me.

"Your time has come. Your time has come," it shouted before flying into my face.

I fell to the ground hard, blood flowing from a deep gash on my forehead. The ridiculous, dive-bombing bird, meanwhile, was writhing in pain on the sidewalk. It looked to me like one of its wings might be broken.

"What's wrong with you," I screamed at the bird.

The crow responded with an ear-piercing shriek, which I took to be a final cry before it died.

"Serves you right," I shouted. "You crazy son-of-a-bitch."

I picked myself up off the stairs and walked toward the crow. I've got you now, I thought, as I watched the bird awkwardly attempt to right itself.

"Your time has come," it said, this time in a quiet, quivering voice.

"I don't think so," I replied. "The tables are turned now."

"Ha ha," laughed the crow.

As I lifted my boot to stomp on the bird's head and shut it up once and for all, I heard what sounded like the roar of an industrial turbine. Turning to see where the sound was coming from, I saw a flock of hundreds of crows swarming as one across the late-afternoon sky. That shriek I'd heard earlier wasn't the bird's death cry. It was a call for help, I realized, as the dark flock descended like a squadron of death angels.

Election Day

When I saw the guns, I knew there was going to be trouble.

The level of discourse between the two candidates had become downright hateful in recent months, and it was even worse among their legions of supporters. That said, the thought of violence never crossed my mind. I figured we'd fall back, as we always had, on the fact that we live in a democracy, one that has managed to peacefully pass the baton from one leader to the next. When it came down to it, our commitment to the greater good – the good of the entire nation – would outweigh our political intolerances. Whether we lean to the left or the right, we're all part of one nation, one nation under God no less.

But that was then and this is now.

A silver pickup truck came to a screeching halt next to

where I was walking. The back of the truck was full of wild-eyed outlaws waving guns. "We're going to City Hall," someone shouted. "Grab your weapon and join us." And with that, they burned rubber and left me petrified on the sidewalk.

My weapon? I wondered. Is that what we've come to?

It was getting dark by the time I arrived home. The power was out. Sirens wailed. There was gunfire. And announcements started coming over the emergency broadcast system. The only time we ever heard the system was during the weekly test every Tuesday. But this wasn't Tuesday. And this wasn't a test.

From my living room window, I could see smoke rising from different areas of the city. I hadn't seen anything like this since the '89 quake. The biggest fire came from the City Hall area, and it wasn't long before an explosion sent a large black cloud into the sky. When the smoke cleared, I saw that City Hall's ornate dome was gone.

Sitting weaponless in my near-dark room, I remembered the old earthquake survival kit my mother had given us when we first moved to the city. It contained a battery-less radio you cranked to power up. I turned the yellow handle, slowly at first and then faster, until I broke through the static.

"Mayhem" … "carnage" … "gunshots … bloodshed." Those were a few of the words I made out on what seemed to be a makeshift news report. After a while, I pieced together that the lawlessness started when the losing candidate refused to concede victory. If that wasn't bad enough, he called upon his followers to take matters into their own hands.

"This is our day," he shouted to them over the static-filled airwaves. "Rise up and take what's ours."

Dark Dream

I dream of a world of darkness where I can't see a thing. I want to sit down somewhere, but it isn't allowed. Instead, I must wander like a blind man, shuffling from one part of the world to the next. It's surprising to me that I never bump into or stumble over anything. Onward I venture, hoping for light.

At some point, I enter a new section of the world where I'm surrounded by sound. It's the sound of pain, and torture, and death. I imagine a Hieronymus Bosch painting come to life through its agonized writhing and bloodcurdling howls. I hear what sounds like the ripping and puncturing and gouging of flesh. I press my hands over my ears, but that doesn't help. I cannot see this world, though my mind makes it visible.

Further along, I hear mechanical noises mixed with the sounds of horror. The rusty hinges of the iron lady. The slow turn of thumbscrews. The thud of the metal truncheon on someone's head. I eventually realize these sounds – as well as the accompanying screams – occur in a continuous loop. I figure this out while standing near the rush of a guillotine, with its heavy blade thumping into the solid wood base after cutting through flesh, and tendons, and bone. Like a kind of insane clockwork, it begins all over again, the fear and terror anew.

When shuffling near what must be the gallows, I hear the release of multiple trap doors, the snap of ropes being pulled taut, and the frantic kicking of legs. It repeats again and again.

My dream has no end. I tell myself to wake up, to leave this place – that it's only a dream after all – but I can't shake free from its slumberous clutches.

It will be light soon, I think, but the daylight never comes. My eyes will become accustomed to the dark is another lie I tell myself. It never happens. Nothing changes. The darkness is eternal. This is my dream, my state of repose, from which I never awaken.

The Vampires' Ball

Invitation in hand, I'm on my way to the vampires' ball.

It's dark outside even with the blood-red moon hanging low over the horizon. It's quiet too, except for the crunch of broken glass under my boots. I can smell the oil from the cars that used to pass through these old corridors of commerce. Prior to the curse, I oversaw security in one of the tallest skyscrapers. It's abandoned now, as are the other structures in this part of the city.

I sense movement in the shadows and a multitude of eyes that watch and wait. Or am I imagining things? When I look, there's nothing. No dogs. No rats. No vampires. And, of course, no people. The truce will keep me safe.

Crossing into what had once been an industrial zone, I bend my ear to catch the faint, lilting strains of classical music. It's a waltz. One-two-three. One-two-three. People used to say this was the wrong side of the tracks, but both sides are equally wrong now. I remember something I haven't thought about for years, a memory of accompanying my mother to her dance lessons. I'd sit in the corner with my comics while she swished across the scuffed-up wooden floor in the arms of the mustachioed dance teacher. One-two-three. One-two-three.

I follow the gentle waves of the waltz music toward my destination, an old brick warehouse originally built for meat packing. The building was shuttered for decades before reopening in the late 1980s as a dance club.

When I stop across the street from the brick building, the music transitions to a pulsing electronic beat, slow at first but then increasing in tempo and volume. The sonic vibration reverberates in my chest and in my throat. Boom. Boom. It goes. Boom. Boom.

In the old days, you would have seen a line of revelers in front of the club and bouncers eager to clear away any sign of trouble. A purple neon light emanates from the crack at the bottom of the door – a sign for me to enter. I hesitate beside a parked car and gaze down at a cracked window. I won't be seeing that again I think when looking at my battle-weary face in the reflection. Tugging down on my collar, I drag my fingers across my neck. That will look different too.

After tonight, it'll all be different.

I spit into the gutter and stride toward the purple neon light of the vampires' ball. The last man is going in.

The Dress

Seeing her again in that dress brought a faint smile of remembrance.

He thought back to the night she first wore the black lace gown to the symphony. The red silk strands interwoven through the fabric gave a crimson sheen to the dress. We didn't normally dress up for the symphony, he remembered. I usually wore jeans and tennis shoes, and she typically went in a casual skirt or pants and a comfortable sweater. But this was our tenth anniversary. We wanted it to be an occasion.

"Let's make it a night to remember," he said. "Fancy clothes. A nice restaurant. A front row seat. Let's see how the other half lives."

"Sounds wonderful," she replied, "But I really don't need to wear an expensive dress." She gave him that look that said "nice idea, honey, but we don't have the money for that kind of extravagance."

"Come on," he pressed. "It's once in a lifetime, right?"

He remembered when she descended the staircase. She'd insisted on keeping the dress a surprise. "It'll be like a wedding dress," she said, and he wondered if she now regretted the fact that they eloped.

She was elegant like a princess making her society debut.

"Aren't you the belle of the ball?" he said when she reached the bottom of the stairs and kissed him on the lips. His friends often joked that he'd been lucky to land such a beauty. On a night like this, he would have to agree.

Sitting in the restaurant, and afterwards as they walked to the concert hall and then to their seats, he saw others watching her, and again he couldn't help but feel like the world's luckiest man. Later that night, he helped her undress. My fingers were shaking, he remembered, like it was our first time.

As the first of the guests arrived at the church, he took a long, last look at his wife. He'd been taken aback when reading her will to find out she wanted an open casket. It didn't come as a surprise, however, that she wanted to be buried in her favorite dress.

Snow Tracks

For nearly three hours the tracks in the snow had been as clear as breadcrumbs leading Little Red Riding Hood to grandma's house in the woods. Then they stopped, as if someone painted the snow with a fresh coat of white paint. Tom looked around and peered ahead at the forest, so dense he couldn't see anything beyond its coniferous edge.

That's where he's waiting for me, thought the lawman.

Tom took a small sip of water from his canteen. It was getting low now, but there was plenty of snow on the ground. "At least I won't die of thirst," he muttered to himself. Food, however, was another matter. Tom patted his heavy coat and felt the lone granola bar in his pocket, deciding to save it for later, even though the rumbling in his belly was getting louder. Because it was habit, he reached for his radio, forgetting for a second that it had died an hour earlier. Tom didn't bother checking his cellphone; he knew there wasn't any connectivity out here.

"Here's another fine mess you've gotten us into," said Tom under his breath.

He didn't know much about the guy he was tracking other than that he was a lifer at Rojas State Prison who pulled off a miraculous escape, like something you'd see in a Hollywood blockbuster. Tom had read the guy's file. He wasn't so different from other criminals, thought Tom, except for the fact that he was jaw-droppingly handsome, like someone you'd see in a magazine ad or a TV commercial.

"This guy should've been in the movies," said Tom. He shook his head, remembering that he was on the trail of a cold-blooded killer. "It's not my job to figure out what makes them tick," he continued, "I'm just here to hunt them down."

The man's a killer, plain and simple, thought Tom. Killing landed him in prison in the first place. And killing busted him out. Those guards – those poor bastards – died in their sleep while Mr. Hollywood slipped into a fresh uniform and strolled out the front gate like he owned the place.

"That's the kind of son-of-a-bitch I'm after," said Tom.

He banged his police radio one more time against his palm to see if it would fire up – no signal. Then he looked around again to see if there was anywhere else the tracks might have led.

There's nowhere else he could have gone, thought Tom as he reached for the Colt .45 in his holster, gritted his teeth, and took his first step in the snow toward the dark edge of the forest.

Waiting at Delirium

I'm waiting for a friend at a bar called Delirium. Even though I'm the only person at the counter, the bartender doesn't seem to be in any hurry to serve me. I'm about to ask her what a guy needs to do to get a drink around here when my "Ride of the Valkyries" ringtone goes off.

"Hey man," says Salty, "I'm running ten minutes late."

That's on top of the ten I've already been waiting, but I don't say anything. We've been friends for a long time, so I'm okay with cutting him some slack.

"See you soon," I say.

Before he hangs up, I catch the sound of the BART announcement in the background, "Walnut Creek station. Next stop, Walnut Creek."

Ten minutes, I think. More like an hour and ten.

The bartender takes her time sauntering over to take my order. She's tattooed up to her neck in Bible verses and sports a nose ring.

"Tequila," I say.

She fills the glass, and I thank her by placing a large tip on the counter. She quickly snatches up the money and returns to the other end of the bar. No smile. No "thank you." Nothing.

Before I can think too much about her rude behavior, an old man pushes through the swinging double doors. With the sun low on the horizon, he's backlit, so I only see the silhouette of his unkempt hair and long, scraggly beard.

"You know the rules, Rasputin," says the bartender. "You're not welcome here."

"Give me a break, Trixie," says the old man. "I need to pee. I need to pee real bad."

"I'm not falling for that line again."

"Really. I gotta go this time. No foolin'."

"You got that right," says Trixie. "You gotta go back out the way you came. You might not remember what happened last time you showed up here, but I sure as hell do. Now get out before I throw you out."

Rasputin spins on his heels and rushes toward the swinging doors.

"I'll get you later, Trixie," he shouts.

"Don't bet on it," she yells back.

He pushes hard on the doors so they slam against the frame.

When it's quiet again, I can't help but ask.

"What'd he do last time he was here?"

I wait for the bartender to say something, anything, but she ignores me. Like I'm not even here. Invisible. I normally wouldn't care, but her rudeness gnaws at me. It's like the rage you get when you're cut off on the freeway. You might let it go once or twice. But it festers and eventually you think enough is enough. Then, when the next person cuts you off, you ride their bumper until they curse the day they ever got their driver's license.

I've reached that sort of agitated state with the bartender. Who does she think she is, treating me like this? What have I ever done to her?

"Correct me if I'm wrong," I say, "but you are trying to make customers feel welcome here, right? Isn't that the whole point of running an establishment like this? Well, isn't it?" On I go, barely stopping to catch my breath.

Trixie the bartender stares me down, her heavily mascaraed eyes drilling into mine like she's about to unleash a stream of venom to surpass my own. When she throws her rag off to the side and walks toward me, I figure I'm about to be kicked out of the bar faster than Rasputin can say "I need to pee."

"You know what, mister?" she says.

"What?"

"You're a real jerk, that's what."

"Well I guess it takes one to know one," I say.

Trixie reaches up to the top shelf and pulls down a bottle of the good stuff. For an instant, I wonder if she's going to crack the bottle over my head. Instead, she opens it and fills my glass.

"You're a real jerk," she says again, "but I like your spunk."

She fills my glass and pours one for herself.

"Here's to you," she says. "Thanks for stopping by."

As we clink our glasses together, "Ride of the Valkyries" sounds again on my phone.

"Hey man." It's Salty. "I'll be another ten minutes."

"Take your time," I tell him. "I don't mind waiting."

We Met in Latin Class

"Amo, Amas, Amat … Amamus, Amatis, Amant."

As we conjugated the verb "to love" during our first day of Latin class who would have thought love really was in the air. I struggled from the start to keep up in the back of the classroom, while the wild-haired woman in the front row of desks spoke Latin as if she hailed from ancient Rome.

One day after class, after working up my courage for weeks, I invited the Latin linguist to join me for a cup of coffee. It wasn't long before we were flipping through our Latin flashcards all over town. From Ocean Beach to North Beach, from the Mission to the Haight, San Francisco became our city of Latin romance.

Our first official date should have clued us in that we were onto something special. I was studying English medieval literature at the time and she was heavily into Dante when we went to a lecture about Chaucer's travels in Italy. Yes, you could say it was a match made in Paradiso.

It's been more than 25 years since we met in Latin class. Though it's been a while since we last conjugated verbs together, we owe everything to the romance that started in that small classroom with those words of love ringing though the air. "Amo, Amas, Amat … Amamus, Amatis, Amant."

And to think some call Latin a dead language.

The Secret of True Happiness™

Jim had never seen anything like it. The crate was filled with hundreds of pieces, each wrapped tightly in plastic and accompanied by its own simple instructions. He picked up a piece and read the note: "Open December 23. Only two more shopping days until Christmas!"

It was January first, so Jim put the piece back in the box.

He peeled off a thin pamphlet marked "Instructions" from the inside lid of the crate. The 16-page booklet contained extensive legal and warranty information and the following instructions in English, Spanish, French, German, Chinese, Japanese, and Tagalog.

Welcome to the Secret of True Happiness!

1. This box contains 365 components. Each one is marked with the day it should be opened.

2. Be sure to open only one component per day.

3. Start on January 1st and proceed to the end of the year. (**Note:** In the event of a leap year, contact the manufacturer for special instructions.)

4. At the end of one year, after you've opened all 365 pieces, you will have unlocked the secret of true happiness.

Jim found the package marked "Open January 1. Happy New Year!" and ripped off the plastic wrap. The package contained a piece of metal, about the size and shape of a half-smoked cigar. Jim shrugged his shoulders. He was unsure what to make of it, but he was also curious about what tomorrow would bring. As he'd soon learn, each metal piece was different from the next. Some were flat and some were round. Some looked like they might be part of a puzzle; others looked like they couldn't possibly fit together with anything else in the crate.

Jim was intrigued at first by the apparent randomness of the metal pieces. He placed each unwrapped object on the kitchen table, thinking he'd soon be assembling a sculpture of some kind. Maybe it would even be a mobile he could hang from the ceiling. By the end of the first month, however, Jim had become frustrated by the fact that the pieces did not fit together, at least not in any way he could figure out. Is this a joke, he wondered? Still, he was determined to see how the mystery played out.

When the components no longer fit on the kitchen table, Jim laid them out on his living room floor. By July, he was no closer to figuring out how the pieces fit together. And he was running out of space inside his small apartment. Even though it was the start of the rainy season, Jim put pieces in his backyard. Fortunately, the metal didn't rust in the rain.

On the last day of the year, Jim picked up the final unwrapped component. The note read, "Open December 31. Congratulations, you now have everything you need for true happiness!" Finally, Jim thought, tearing at the plastic wrapping. He was ready for the "ah-ha" moment – that instant when all would be revealed.

The final piece was a small pyramid-shaped object. Jim rotated it in his hand. He squinted and rubbed his forehead, but he still couldn't figure out the mystery of the metal pieces. He scanned the rest of his collection, from the first half-smoked cigar on his kitchen table, to the clutter of dusty pieces on his living room floor, to the last four months' worth of stuff scattered across his backyard. It wasn't a puzzle or a sculpture or a mobile of any kind. It was just 365 random pieces of junk.

Jim felt the rage come upon him all at once. He dropped the metal pyramid and smashed it under his boot. He then gathered up all the pieces on the kitchen table in a large tablecloth and flung the entire bundle out into the yard. Next, he stomped on the components on his living room floor before hurling them all outside. Lastly, Jim lifted the cardboard crate. The secret of true happiness, he thought. Yeah right! What did I miss? he asked himself. *What did*

I miss? He flipped over the crate, shook it violently, and gave one final thwack to the bottom of the box.

The instruction pamphlet dropped onto the kitchen floor.

Jim tossed the crate off to the side and picked up the thin manual, flipping through the English, Spanish, French, German, Chinese, Japanese, and Tagalog instructions for the missing clue. Any clue! That's when he noticed a note on the back cover. In the finest of fine print, it read:

HAPPINESS is all around us.
No Assembly Required.

The Secret of True Happiness™
Developed by Obsessive Gimmicks, Inc.
San Francisco, California. U.S.A.
Manufactured in China.

Acknowledgments

Special thanks to the following for their contributions.

Alan Beatts at Borderlands Books. For sharing his wisdom.

Elizabeth Bernstein. For her writing workshops at The Grotto.

Jennie Bitner. For her writing workshops at The Grotto.

Dan Davis. For his careful reading.

Kathy Garlick. For her writing workshop at the Writing Salon.

Chris Held. For designing the interior pages.

Henrik Kam. For the photo of the author.

Rosalie Lack. For everything.

Monica Pasqual. For her songwriting workshops.

Aimee Stevland. For the cover design.

About the Author

Photo by Henrik Kam

Greg Roensch is a writer who lives in San Francisco, California. In addition to owning a writing and editing business (Six String Communications), Greg writes travel articles, short stories, and songs. This is his first collection of short, short stories.

Contact him at www.gregroensch.com.